An Irresistible Woman

Something about the way Charlotte was staring at his mouth and the languid drift of her gaze back up to his eyes made him see her—not as a patient and not as an innocent he'd just vowed to protect—but as a woman.

A beautiful woman.

A desirable woman.

For the first time in his life, Travis almost wished he *were* a rake. In that moment, with the sea breeze gently blowing her dark curls, her dreamy eyes fixed on his, her delicate shoulders dwarfed beneath the oversized sailor's coat, he wanted naught more than to plant a long, lingering kiss on her alluring mouth.

Cover design by Richard Campbell
Dress photo, hair, make-up and gown courtesy of Matti's Millinery & Costumes of www.mattionline.com
Formatting by Author E.M.S.

Glynnis Campbell – Publisher
P.O. Box 341144
Arleta, California 91331
Contact: glynnis@glynnis.net

ISBN-10: 1-63480-057-5
ISBN-13: 978-1-63480-057-0

Published in the United States of America.

THE
STOWAWAY

THE PREQUEL NOVELLA TO CALIFORNIA LEGENDS

OTHER BOOKS BY GLYNNIS CAMPBELL

THE WARRIOR MAIDS OF RIVENLOCH
The Shipwreck (novella)
A Yuletide Kiss (short story)
Lady Danger
Captive Heart
Knight's Prize

THE WARRIOR DAUGHTERS OF RIVENLOCH
The Storming (novella)
A Rivenloch Christmas (short story)
Bride of Fire
Bride of Ice
Bride of Mist

THE KNIGHTS OF DE WARE
The Handfasting (novella)
My Champion
My Warrior
My Hero

ACKNOWLEDGMENTS

A special thank you to my shipmate Lauren Royal, who suggested a cruise just when I needed it most;

Holland America Cruise Line, which, by pure serendipity, featured 19th century ship models and orchids on board;

My sister Jewel authors, Cheryl Bolen, Erica Ridley, Brenda Hiatt, and Darcy Burke, for inviting me into their Regency world for a brief visit;

Amy, Kirby, and Jill, expert time jugglers;

The real Travis Jameson, for letting me borrow his uber-cool name;

and Tatiana Maslany and Nikolaj Coster-Waldau for their inspiration.

For the America I know and love,
where science is welcomed with open arms
and new beginnings are possible

CHAPTER 1

THE DE WARE MANOR HOUSE
NEAR EDINBURGH, SCOTLAND
OCTOBER 1810

"**D**amn, George! Are ye sure ye want to do this?"

"'Tis a rather large sum, old boy."

"Aye, and ye're already down a wee fortune."

Charlotte knew it wasn't proper to eavesdrop. The young gentlemen had retired to the library after dinner. They expected privacy. It was none of a lady's affair what the brandy-and-cigar set did while the females were left to their own devices in the drawing room.

Unfortunately for Charlotte, those feminine devices included chattering endlessly on and on. About the latest fashions in London. The romantic eligibility of various Edinburgh bachelors. And who'd been invited to which Christmas ball. All of which she found incredibly shallow and deadly dull.

Besides, as her father oft remarked, Charlotte had been born with inexorable curiosity. It was that curiosity that gave her a scientific mind. And sometimes got her into more than a wee bit of trouble.

She'd excused herself from the ladies, ostensibly to powder her nose, mostly to give her ears a rest. But as she breezed past the library, she couldn't help but be intrigued by the conversation drifting through the open crack of the door.

Hearing her brother George's name, she naturally felt compelled to stop and apprise herself of the situation.

Their parents had gone to Oxford to visit her oldest brother, William, at university. The second oldest, John, was an officer in the Navy, fighting in the Baltic Sea. In their absence, George had been left in charge of the household.

Despite her brother being only a year older than she, Charlotte was well aware that George and Responsibility weren't the best of companions. Thus, she felt it was her duty to make sure Tragedy didn't ensue.

Even if that involved a bit of subterfuge and listening at doors.

Tucking a stray lock of her short brown curls under her bandeau, she peered through the crack of the door,

searching the group of lounging dandies until she spotted George at cards.

Cigar smoke hovered like a halo over the six young gentlemen at the rosewood card table. But they hardly looked angelic. Their jackets were slung over the backs of their chairs. Their white sleeves were rolled up and their cravats undone. Brandy sparkled in their cut crystal rummers. They slouched over a game of *vingt-et-un*.

Charlotte narrowed her eyes in disapproval. Every night this week, George had met with his friends to play cards—drinking, smoking, and gambling long into the wee hours. It seemed her brother was intent on squeezing all the debauchery he could into the weeks their parents were away.

She wouldn't have minded if the games were a casual entertainment. But George seemed to be obsessed with wagering of late. Eager to play. Feverish to win.

If he wasn't careful…

George took a swig of brandy and slammed down the empty glass, motioning for a servant to refill his rummer.

"Are ye in or out, lads?" he challenged, his words slurred by drink. "Put up your damned markers."

"Not so fast, old boy," the *banquier* warned, placing a hand on George's forearm. "Are ye sure ye're good for the wager?"

Righteous indignation crackled off George like lightning as he cast off the *banquier*'s hand. He snarled, "O' course I'm good for it! I'm a bloody de Ware, aren't I?"

His vehement outburst silenced the room. Charlotte bit her lip. She felt sorry for her brother, even though he could be a complete cad when he'd been drinking. George was embarrassing himself in front of his peers.

In the next moment, he seemed to realize that. One corner of his lip curled up in a mischievous grin, and his eyes twinkled as he glanced around the library—at the distinguished portraits on the wall, the shelves full of leather-bound books, the gilt mahogany furnishings. "Ach! I'm growin' weary o' this shabby hovel anyway."

His jest broke the uncomfortable silence and made everyone laugh. Everyone but Charlotte. She found no humor in the notion of George gambling away their home.

A young man warming his hands by the fire called out, "Well, if ye happen to lose it all, Georgie, I know a lady who'll keep ye in fine style for five years at least."

A conspiratorial "ooh" circled the room.

"As a concubine?" George asked, stroking his chin as if considering the option.

"Nay," the man replied. "As an indentured servant."

More laughter filled the room, disgusting Charlotte. Debt was not a laughing matter. She knew of more

than one family that had been ruined by gambling debt, forced to sell off their possessions, one by one.

The *banquier* tapped his finger on the table. "Let's see what we've all got then, gents."

Charlotte held her breath as the players began to reveal their hands.

Then, just as George was reaching to flip over his card, Humphries the butler barked out behind her. "Miss!"

She gasped and whirled around.

They both knew what she'd been doing.

His eyes were flat with disapproval.

Her face was pink with guilt.

But the servant was wise enough not to scold her.

And she was wise enough not to try to explain.

He cleared his throat. "The ladies are inquiring about your absence, Miss."

"I was just on my way back."

He gave a nod of his head. "Very good, Miss." He reached past her and silently closed the door.

Charlotte smoothed her rose satin gown, which she realized probably matched her face at the moment. Trying to salvage her dignity, she walked toward the drawing room.

Somehow, she managed to fritter away another hour, pretending to enjoy the inane conversation. As usual, she failed to engage any of the women in her own topic of interest—botany.

Once the purview of females, botany had fallen out of favor with proper ladies. Prudish Johann Siegesbeck had deemed the sexual classification of flowers "loathsome harlotry," too offensive to a woman's delicate sensibilities. What might have been common ground in years past was now considered outré by decent society.

And so, as always, Charlotte ended up having little to say and was left feeling awkward. Out of step. And socially exhausted.

It had been George's idea to have his university friends over this eve, dignifying the gathering by including several of their sisters. Thus it had fallen to Charlotte to serve as hostess, no matter how much she resented the task.

She'd much rather have spent the evening studying the Caledonian Horticultural Society report. The latest installment had arrived this afternoon and was sitting on her father's desk, unread.

The report was sent to her father after every meeting. Not because Charles de Ware was interested in horticulture. In all honesty, he couldn't tell a dandelion from a daisy.

But Charlotte's application for membership in the newfound Caledonian Horticultural Society had been turned down. Not because she was a hobbyist. The Society was accepting those with or without formal education. It had been turned down because she was a woman.

Her father would hear none of that. Refusing to bow to what he deemed archaic rules, he promptly gave a hefty donation to the Society, obliging them to send him the notes from their meetings, which he then handed over to Charlotte.

Charlotte looked forward to perusing the report. Though it dealt mostly with crops and propagation, horticulture was a world she understood. Reading the latest discoveries made her feel like part of the scientific community.

Sadly, by the time the gentlemen came round to collect the ladies, the night was half gone. Charlotte's smile was worn thin with overuse. Her eyes drooped like the petals of an overwatered rose.

She bid the guests goodnight and dismissed Mrs. Scott, telling her she could clean up in the morning— an order the fastidious housekeeper predictably refused. When Charlotte finally mounted the stairs to her bedroom, she found her brother had already retired. She'd have to wait until tomorrow to learn how he'd fared at cards.

Charlotte woke long before George, of course. After his night of carousing, she imagined her brother would sleep till afternoon.

She threw on her white muslin morning dress, splashed water on her face, and raked back her unruly mop of dark curls. Then, snapping up the notebook she kept by her bed, she hurried to the first of the three south-facing windows, which were lined with flowerpots.

She smiled in satisfaction. The sky was cloudless. Her plants would get a good drenching of sunlight today.

She was aware her collection of two dozen specimens of *Orchidaceae* was impressive. The fact that she'd managed to keep the tropical flowers alive and blooming, some for as long as fifteen years, was even more remarkable, given the inhospitable clime of Scotland.

To a wee lass, the colorful flowers had been treasures her Grandfather de Ware brought back for her from the exotic places he sailed. With every ocean voyage he took, he collected a plant for her. Soon she'd acquired an assortment of beautiful blooms in every color of the rainbow.

When her father obtained the translated volumes of Linnaeus' *A System of Vegetables* for his library, she began to learn the taxonomy of the flowers she possessed.

And two years ago, when he'd gifted her a copy of Olof Swartz's *Genera Orchidacearum* for her birthday, she'd been able to finely tune that identification and classification of the various genera and species.

Only then did she realize what a true treasure they were.

Stopping at the first flower, the *Oncidium punchellum* with its lavender *labellum* and maroon guide markings,

she turned the pot to count the blooms and check for new growth.

Some orchids went dormant in autumn. But those of the *Oncidium* genus flourished in winter. Sure enough, a new nub of a rhizome protruded perhaps two millimeters off the base of the stem.

She carefully dug her finger into the soil at the edge of the pot, checking the level of moisture.

Outdoors, the flowers would never have thrived. The weather was too cold and rainy. Tropical orchids preferred lots of sunlight, just enough humidity to keep the roots damp, and at least a modicum of warmth. She found keeping them on the windowsill was ideal for protecting them against chill and dehydration.

It took her nearly an hour to record her daily observations. But it always thrilled her when she could measure the slow progress of a plant, catalog the birth and death of a blossom, and, best of all, witness the surprising revelation of an orchid's first bloom.

She'd already filled several books with meticulous notes and sketches. They were observations nobody but she had ever read. Observations nobody would *ever* read, she supposed.

Yet she'd always sensed that her notes were somehow important. That they would one day be of use. She considered it her scientific duty to record each day's statistics. Even when it meant missing breakfast and having to raid the kitchen for a mid-morning roll with marmalade.

Because most of the plants were dormant at this time of year, she fulfilled her obligations in short order. She managed to take her morning tea and toast well before noon. Then she went to her father's study to fetch the Caledonian Horticultural Society's report, bringing it to the drawing room to read.

Some hours later, lost in an article on the cultivation of French pears, she nearly jumped off the settee when Humphries suddenly appeared with a silver tray.

"The post, Miss," he announced. "Shall I...?"

Before Humphries had to face the uncomfortable decision of whether to hand the day's post to *her* instead of the Man of the House, George came hurtling down the stairs.

"I'll take that, Humphries," he said.

George looked dreadful. His valet had managed to dress him in a clean shirt and breeches and comb his hair. But his skin had a pale cast, almost like the color of her *Vanilla planifolia* orchid, and his hands were shaking as he reached out for the letter on the tray. His eyes were rimmed with red, and there were dark circles around them, as if he'd lain awake all night.

She waited until Humphries was gone to address him in concern. "Are ye feelin' well, George?"

"Aye. Fine."

Shuffling through the envelopes, he selected one and stared at the thing, as if he were afraid to open it.

"What is it?" She lowered the report to her lap. "Not the Navy?" she asked, her heart in her throat. She frequently worried about her brother John, away at war.

"Nay," he muttered, "'tis just business."

She lifted a brow. Business? George? That was news to her. George didn't seem to be interested in business of any kind.

George, still staring at the envelope, wiped away the sweat above his lip with the back of his fingers.

Disturbed by his sickly appearance, Charlotte rose from the settee. "Perhaps ye should have somethin' to eat, George. 'Twill make ye feel—"

"I don't need anythin' to eat," he snapped. Then, remembering his manners, he lowered his eyes. "Thank ye for the offer," he murmured. "I'll be fine. I'm just tired."

No doubt, she thought, considering he'd been up until all hours of the night, five nights in a row. Too much brandy had likely taken its toll as well. Then she recalled the conversation she'd overheard in the library.

Was it possible George had had a round of bad luck? Had he overplayed his hand? Was he in trouble?

"I'll be in the library," he said, never meeting her eyes. "I'll take tea in there."

"George," she called out as he turned to go.

"Aye?" he said over his shoulder.

One had to be delicate about these things.

"Did ye...enjoy the evenin'?"

He shrugged. "As much as any."

She forced a nervous chuckle to her lips. "Ye didn't gamble away my dowry, did ye?"

He stiffened. For one awful instant, Charlotte wondered if he'd done just that.

But in the next moment, his shoulders dropped, and he turned to her with his familiar cheeky grin. "Why? Ye have a husband lined up, do ye?"

George could always make her laugh. "Hardly." She had yet to meet a man who wasn't either intimidated or repulsed by her scientific pursuits. And unless and until she did, marriage seemed like an undesirable ambition.

"Well then..." He turned away, heading down the hall toward the library. "As a matter o' fact," he called out, "things worked out quite well. I'm out o' debt and back in the game."

She frowned as he closed the library door behind him. *Back in the game.* That didn't sound good. She was hoping his brush with financial ruin would cure his fever for cards.

Whatever business George had in the library occupied him all afternoon.

Charlotte, donning a chip straw bonnet and old half boots and tying an apron over her morning dress, spent most of the day outdoors.

From the time she'd been young, the things growing in the garden had fascinated her. She'd spent hours collecting seeds, dissecting flowers, and pollinating plants by hand.

Today was no different. She made sketches of bulging rose hips, cutting one in half to examine the interior layers. She harvested the strange curly seeds of the *Calendula officinalis*, marigold, slipping them into a paper envelope for safekeeping. She wished to study whether they would germinate if stored for one year, two years, or more. Then, feeling ambitious, she used a trowel to unearth several of the *Lilium* bulbs for study, dividing and replanting the rest.

So distracted was she that she missed her afternoon tea and had to rush into her *Narcissus jonquilla*-colored silk gown for supper. When she arrived at the table, Humphries indicated with a critical arch of his brow that, despite thoroughly washing her hands, there was still a thin rim of dirt under her nails.

She didn't care. In fact, she would just as soon dine in the garden in her boots and apron. It seemed wasteful to her to make so many changes of clothing, especially when the only other person at the table was George. And despite the talented Mrs. Abernathy and her sumptuous courses, Charlotte would have been just as happy with bread and cheese, especially since, for the first time in days, there were no guests to feed.

Despite—or perhaps because of—George's unhealthy pallor, he ate only half his supper before he laid the napkin down on the table.

"I've had a letter from Father," he said, waiting to catch her eye.

She looked up, holding her fork full of minced collops aloft. "Aye?"

He glanced at his claret. Picked up the glass. Brought it toward his mouth. Changed his mind. Put it back down.

"There's been a wee change o' plans."

"Mm?" She slipped the fork into her mouth, chewing the rich bits of beef.

"It seems they won't be comin' home for the holidays after all."

Her brows popped up. She set her fork down on the plate and swallowed the collops.

"But what about the ball?" For as long as she could remember, the de Wares had hosted a grand Christmas ball.

George raised his glass again. This time he finished off the claret.

Suddenly, Charlotte had an awful thought. "They're not expectin' us to host the Christmas ball, are they?" Her stomach tightened with dread.

"Nay."

She breathed a sigh of relief. "Then what?"

"We've been asked to spend Christmas with kin."

"What kin? Not Aunt Effie?" While Aunt Effie was a sweet old bird, she lived in a drafty estate in the Highlands. Besides, she was as dotty as a ladybug.

"Nay," he said. "'Tis a cousin...abroad."

"Abroad?" She wasn't aware they had any kin abroad. Maybe a relative from Norman times who still lived in France. But the French and Scottish weren't exactly on friendly terms at the moment. "Abroad where?"

He lifted his glass again, forgetting it was empty. When he set it back down, he stared at the stem, twisting it between his fingers.

"America."

"America!" Her shriek rang out in the dining room.

At her outburst, Humphries poked his head in to see what was amiss. Satisfied that no mayhem had ensued, he sighed and closed the door again.

"America?" she repeated in a whisper.

George scraped back his chair to reach for the decanter of claret in the middle of the table. He unstopped it and poured himself a second glass.

"What kin do we have in America?" she asked.

He sat, gazing into his glass a long while before taking another drink. "Mrs. Smith. Mrs. Eugenia Smith."

"Who?"

"She's a...distant cousin o' Mother's, a widow."

Charlotte blinked in surprise. This was the first she'd heard of cousin Eugenia.

George added, "Father thought 'twould be good for us to meet the New York branch o' the family."

"New York?"

A tingling started in her veins. Christmas in New York?

Suddenly she didn't care if Mrs. Eugenia Smith was the half-sister of her third cousin, twice removed. She'd leap at the chance to go to New York.

New York, after all, was the location of the Elgin Botanic Garden.

Since she was a young lass, when Professor David Hosack had first planted the public garden, it had been a dream of Charlotte's to see the amazing place. But she'd always considered it an unachievable dream, as likely as becoming Queen or owning an elephant.

The idea it might be possible thrilled and excited her.

"We're goin' to New York?" she asked breathlessly.

"Aye."

"Ye're serious?"

She sincerely hoped this wasn't one of George's nasty jests. That he wouldn't suddenly burst out in laughter at how gullible his wee sister was. Because if it *was* a jest, it would be too cruel for words.

"Aye." He *looked* serious. Not even a hint of humor lurked in his eyes.

"But this is wonderful!" she burst out.

"'Tis?"

"O' course, ye silly. New York is where the Elgin Botanic Garden is."

"Oh, aye," he seemed to remember. "Ye've always longed to go there, aye?"

Her eyes lit up. "And maybe we can visit Columbia College." David Hosack had once been the Professor of Botany at the esteemed college. "New York," she sighed.

"So ye *want* to go?" George acted surprised, but she was sure he was teasing her.

"O' course I want to go! Who wouldn't want to go to America?" Unable to contain her excitement, she got up from the table and began pacing. "But truly, George? We're truly goin' to New York?"

"There's a ship leavin' in three days."

"Three days!" she exclaimed, halting in her tracks. "'Tis hardly time to pack. Only three days?"

"Aye." George seemed unusually calm, considering the adventure they were about to undertake. She blamed it on his overindulgence in brandy last night. "Eight o'clock sharp on Monday mornin'."

She resumed pacing, caught up in a flurry of plans and possibilities. There was little time to prepare.

"I'll have to pack straightaway." Then she hesitated. "How many servants will we take?"

"Servants." He winced. "I don't think we'll have room for any servants. The ship's bound to be tight quarters. We'll have to manage on our own. Do ye think ye can do that?"

Charlotte nodded. Then the reality of the voyage hit her with sudden clarity. Squealing in excitement, she rushed over to George and wrapped her arms about his neck.

"Oh, Georgie, 'twill be a real adventure, won't it? Just ye and me on an ocean voyage, off to explore a new world."

Amused and annoyed by her familiarity, George pried her arms loose. "Go on now." His voice was gruff, but full of brotherly fondness. "And only pack what ye need," he called after her as she rushed from the library. "No more than three or four trunks."

That would do fine. She could stuff her gowns and hats into one trunk, her slippers, pelisses, and research books into another. That would leave two trunks for her orchids.

She had no intention of leaving them behind. Humphries and Mrs. Scott might be able to manage the house well enough while she was away. But no one could manage her collection of plants with the care and attention they required.

Fortunately, when her grandfather retired from his voyages abroad, he gave her his copy of *Directions for Bringing Over Seeds and Plants from the East-Indies and Other Distant Countries in a State of Vegetation.* She knew just how to pack her precious flowers for the journey.

It took a full day to have the special trunks built. They were three feet long, one foot wide and two feet

high, with a six-inch shelf along the bottom and ventilation slots on the ends.

The next day she carefully repotted the *Orchidacaea*, wrapping each ball of roots in wet *Sphagnum palustre* moss, stringing pack-thread between each plant to stabilize it, and tucking more moss into the crevices to insulate the plants.

Then, after she tossed her clothes and shoes and fripperies into the remaining two trunks, she tucked in a few of her most precious botany volumes and several spare notebooks to record her observations.

If her brother was rather quiet, Charlotte took no special notice of it, other than to be relieved he wasn't wasting his coin at cards. She was too excited about the journey ahead to pay him much mind. Indeed, the night before they were due to embark, she was almost too excited to sleep.

CHAPTER 2

The five young surgeons stood around the pine trunk, speaking in fretful whispers.

"Are ye sure?"

"That he's goin' to be vexed? Oh, aye!"

"Nay! Are ye sure he can breathe?"

"O' course…I think."

"He'll be fine. The planks on the back side o' the crate are riddled with knotholes."

"And the *principium somniferum* ye gave him—'tis safe?"

"Safer than pure opium."

One of them sighed. "I still don't think this is a good idea."

"'Tisn't like he's given us any choice."

"Aye, that's for certain. The poor chap's not cut out

for duelin'. In any case, he wouldn't have survived another year, basket-makin' with every stray strumpet that—"

"Hell and the devil!"

"Sorry. But if he doesn't stop carryin' on, he'll be dead ere Christmas."

The five young men were silent as they gazed down at the sixth, crammed into the trunk in naught but his smallclothes.

"He just looks so...helpless."

"He looks dead. Are we sure he's not dead?"

One of them lifted Travis's limp hand, feeling for his pulse. "Slow, but strong as ever," he proclaimed.

"The effects should wear off in six hours or so."

"Dash it all, he'll be furious."

"A pity we couldn't dress him properly."

"There was no time. Besides, 'tis the least o' his troubles."

"He'll live out the day. 'Tis what matters most."

They all nodded in agreement.

"Bon voyage, old boy."

They lowered the lid, intentionally busting off the latch.

A pound note insured the ship's bracket-faced chief officer asked no questions when they brought the trunk on board at the crack of dawn. And the name printed on the lid—MR. REGINALD JAMESON—assured the safe delivery of its contents.

Charlotte pulled the fur-trimmed pelisse—in a blue that matched her eyes—tighter around her. A chill breeze was coming off the sea, but she could scarcely contain her rapture as she watched the sun rise from the weather deck of *The Fortuity*. She and George had arrived early to stow their trunks. It was still hard to believe this packet ship was going to be her home for the next six weeks or so.

She expected they'd be housed in one of the eight staterooms reserved for travelers of quality, cabins that opened onto the saloon for dining.

But the captain, recognizing their distinguished family name, had instead offered one of his own three staterooms at the stern of the ship.

Though relatively lavish, the cabin was small, no more than ten feet square. A gold and scarlet Axminster rug filled the space, which also included a sturdy bed with a brocade burgundy spread, a cherry wood dressing table and armoire, a flowered porcelain wash basin, a gold-upholstered settee, and two matched chairs. Charlotte was pleased to discover the cabin was on the port side of the ship. Its four decent-sized windows would be south-facing for most of their journey. On bright days, she could open the lid of her special trunks and let her orchids drink in the sunlight.

George didn't share her enthusiasm for the journey. He seemed dour and terse this morning. She supposed he was pining over the card games he would miss.

Or the friends he was leaving behind.

Or the access to unlimited bottles of claret he'd no longer have.

Whatever it was, once they were settled in, George encouraged her to explore the vessel. Since they'd be sharing the cabin, with George using the settee for sleeping, he intended to speak to someone about hanging a curtain for privacy.

Meanwhile, she watched with fascination as the crew readied the ship to sail, dragging ropes to and fro, hauling trunks of goods, barrels of beer and water, and crates of flapping chickens and geese up the gangplank. Though she saw a dozen or so stateroom passengers file on board, *The Fortuity* was mostly a merchant vessel. According to the captain, it would deliver wool and finished cotton cloth to America and return to Britain with tobacco, raw cotton, sugar, and rice.

The sun was glinting off the gentle waves of the harbor, warming Charlotte's brow, when the last of the passengers finally boarded.

George had not returned. Perhaps he was still arranging the stateroom. It was a shame he'd miss the ship's launch.

Children with their nurses waved from the dock. A few matrons dabbed at their eyes with handkerchiefs, bidding their loved ones farewell. The captain barked out orders as broad-backed sailors weighed anchor.

Then Charlotte's eye was caught by something small and dark weaving through the people at the dock. A scruffy black dog. Full of self-importance and on a serious mission, the wee terrier sniffed along the wooden planks, likely on the trail of some unlucky rodent. It stopped to bark, and she grinned when each powerful "woof" made its feet lift off the ground.

The crew began untying the mooring line, allowing the ship to slowly ease away from the dock. The poor dog started shifting frantically back and forth, barking in panic.

Then, to the crew's consternation and Charlotte's alarm, just as the gangplank was hauled halfway in, the terrier took a daring leap over the water. While Charlotte watched with bated breath, the stubby-legged pup caught the end of the plank, scrambling its way atop the boards. It raced up the length of the gangplank, dodging the sailors' attempts to catch it, and sprang onto the deck of the ship.

Before anyone could stop the slippery rascal, the dog bolted down the midship stairs to the lower deck.

Now, even if the terrier could be retrieved, it would be too late to toss him back onto shore.

The sailors seemed to know this.

"We've got a stowaway!" one of them joked.

"Well, he'd better earn his keep."

"And he'd better stay out o' the stores."

"The stores? He'd better stay out o' the captain's rum."

There was laughter all around. Charlotte supposed they weren't too upset to have a terrier on board a ship. They were skilled mouse-hunters after all.

She couldn't help but wonder, however, if the poor thing belonged to someone who would miss it.

Then, before she could fret too much about it, she was distracted by the curious shifting under her feet. They were truly free of their mooring now and underway.

Once the sails were unfurled, the ship moved through the harbor like a grand old dame across a ballroom, with stately elegance, swaying slightly from side to side.

Charlotte was mildly irritated that George was missing the sights. He would have enjoyed this unfamiliar waterside view of the royal burgh they knew and loved. The shore drifted past, its banks populated by storehouses, piers, and dozens of sailing vessels of all shapes and sizes.

Nearly an hour passed before *The Fortuity* left the protected harbor at Leith to venture into the open sea. More sails were unfurled. The water grew rougher. And what had been a cool breeze became a chilling wind that tangled her hair and buffeted her cheeks.

Gathering her pelisse about her, she made her way toward the stairs that led to the lower deck. She clung to the rail so she wouldn't lose her footing as the ship

tilted. A crewman helped her descend the shallow steps.

She expected George would be in their stateroom, either hanging the privacy curtain or sleeping off another late night of drinking.

But he wasn't there. And no curtain had been hung. He hadn't even moved the settee. Where could he have gone?

She waited for him in the cabin, using the time to record her *Orchidacaea* observations, a task made difficult by the listing of the ship. She theorized that their growth while aboard the ship would be erratic. They'd been uprooted from the environment to which they were accustomed, after all.

Rather like Charlotte herself.

When she finished and George still wasn't back, she began searching for him. She scoured the entire main deck. She inquired at the maproom, the boatswain's cabin, and the carpenter's cabin. She even peered in at the galley, where the cook was preparing a mouth-watering pork roast.

She took a quick inventory of the weather deck above, where, now that they were in the open sea, no one but the ship's crew had the fortitude and sea legs to stride easily from bow to stern. Young lads climbed into the rigging like monkeys and trimmed the sails with expert skill, while Charlotte had to cling to whatever railing or post she could reach for balance.

George wasn't there.

He certainly wasn't swimming in the bilge water below decks.

So unless he'd stumbled upon a card game in one of the other passenger's cabins, there was only one place he could be. The hold.

Normally, passengers like Charlotte would never venture into the hold. The goods stored there were the responsibility of the captain until the ship arrived at port. And some of those goods were quite valuable. Until they reached America, they were his property, and the hold was his domain.

But curious Charlotte seldom let rules prevent her.

George was missing. She had to locate him.

If she got caught, she would simply plead ignorance. There were advantages to being perceived to be a featherbrained female.

Finding the door unguarded, she crept into the forbidden interior, securing the door behind her.

The hold was dim, lit by two small portholes. It took a moment for her eyes to adjust to the dark. Pallets, boxes, casks, and trunks were stacked ceiling-high, secured to the bulkheads with rope. Bags of grain slouched in one corner. Bottles shivered against each other in divided crates.

As the ship labored through the waves, the wood creaked, and the waves slapped against the bulkheads.

The odors of brine, oil, and hemp lingered in the stale air of the close quarters.

A quick assessment told her George wasn't here.

But she wasn't alone in the hold. Sitting beside one of the crates, staring up at her with big black eyes, was the intrepid stowaway terrier.

She had to smile. The wicked imp looked none the worse for his risky flight. She crouched down to take a closer look.

"Good mornin', wee one," she murmured.

The pup came to his feet. But he didn't wag his tail. Instead, he regarded her with suspicion.

"Who do ye belong to, eh?" She clucked her tongue. "Someone's bound to miss a handsome fellow like ye."

Sensing she was no threat, the dog sank onto his hindquarters again. Then he lowered farther to rest his head on his paws.

Charlotte pursed her lips in empathy. She couldn't just leave the sad creature here in the hold. It seemed a clean enough animal. It was neither mangy nor starving. It wasn't a stray. It clearly belonged to someone.

Perhaps she'd keep the pup in her cabin. She could save morsels of food from her plate to feed it. And at night it could snuggle at the foot of her bed.

"How would ye like to come with me?" she asked, reaching out for him.

He lifted his head and began growling at Charlotte.

She prudently withdrew her hands, promising, "I won't hurt ye, lad. I'll only keep ye safe till we can find your proper home."

She wondered if he even *had* a proper home anymore. The captain certainly wouldn't be turning the ship around to return him. And if he'd left family behind in Edinburgh, she doubted the owners would pay for the dog's passage back from America.

On the other hand, perhaps he belonged to someone on board.

"Come with me," she said, reaching out again. "Maybe we can find your owner."

He didn't growl this time. But he stood his ground, refusing to budge, staring at her in somber stubbornness.

She sighed. Then she had an idea. "Hey, wee fellow, how would ye like a nice bit o' roast pork?"

Perhaps she could lure him away with the promise of a meal.

As if he understood, he licked his chops. But when she stood up, trying to coax him to come with her, he laid his head back down in regret.

She glanced at the trunk beside which the terrier was stationed. He seemed to be standing guard over it.

She narrowed her eyes at the name burned into the large pine box.

MR. REGINALD JAMESON.

The name was unfamiliar to her. And she knew most of the important families in Edinburgh.

MR. REGINALD JAMESON.

That was it. No residence. No further shipping information.

Then she calculated the size of the crate. Her eyes widened.

She'd heard tales of dogs visiting their master's graves, sitting there for days without food or water, waiting for the master to return.

Was the pup's owner dead?

Good heavens! Was Mr. Reginald Jameson's dead body in that trunk?

She gasped in horror.

Which startled a sharp bark out of the dog.

Which startled a foul word out of Charlotte.

"Shh!" she cautioned herself and the dog, wondering if she could whisk the beast away before he started making enough fuss to...wake the dead.

The terrier started pawing at the crate and whining.

Charlotte grimaced. Now what was she to do?

She wanted to get out of there with all haste. But not without the pup.

If the sailors discovered the dog had no owner—at least not one who was living—they might just toss him overboard.

She couldn't let that happen.

"Come on, lad," she murmured, eager to get as far away from Mr. Reginald Jameson as possible. "I'm afraid your master's not comin' home. I fear he's gone to heaven." Even as she said the words, she wasn't so sure. After all, what kind of cad would die and leave such an adorable wee pet behind to fend for itself?

The dog scraped at the trunk again and gave two curt barks.

And then the trunk budged.

CHAPTER 3

Travis Jameson couldn't open his eyes. His lids were too heavy. His tongue felt thick in his mouth. And his limbs ached as if someone had tied them in a knot.

In the distance, as if he were dreaming it, he heard Campbell bark.

Damn it, he had to wake up.

He was breathing, thank God, though the air felt close, stagnant. He could vaguely sense his heart pumping in his chest. But something was making him lethargic, paralyzing him.

Had he been drugged?

He tried to remember.

But it was all too much effort.

It was so much easier to drift off on a cloud of numb surrender.

Campbell was whining now, nagging Travis to take him for a walk.

Travis knew too well the consequences of ignoring Campbell's demands. He'd had to clean up more than one mess in the house.

He tried to rouse himself. And failed.

Then he heard a muffled feminine voice.

Gradually, like an image under the lens of a microscope, wisps of memory came slowly into focus.

Sir Wyndham. Travis had been caught with Sir Wyndham's wife. Now he remembered.

Sir Wyndham had returned early from his London trip to discover his wife half-naked in their bed and Travis in his bedroom. Things had gone rapidly from bad to worse.

Lady Wyndham, of course, could not defend Travis. Nor would Travis allow her to try.

There had been angry words. Accusations. And finally, a challenge. A duel with pistols at dawn.

Travis had had no choice but to accept. To do anything less would have stained Lady Wyndham's honor.

When his friends found out, they dragged Travis to The White Hart to spend what everyone was sure would be his last night on earth at the bottom of a tankard.

But then what had happened?

It was all a fog.

Campbell barked again. This time, Travis shook the cobwebs from his brain and banged his head against something hard. He managed to pry open his eyelids. But it didn't matter much. It was still as dark as night. Maybe it still *was* night.

Where was he?

He tried to move. Half of his body felt numb, nerveless. The other half tingled with the painful recovery of sensation.

In the next instant, three things happened.

He discovered he was unable to move more than a few inches in any direction, trapped in some kind of wooden enclosure.

The awful fear that it might be a coffin brought him fully alert.

And panic made him surge upward to burst out of his prison, wrenching the lid half off its hinges.

He blinked, shielding his eyes against the sudden light with his arm.

He was in a ship's hold.

Campbell was skittering happily before him, his tail wagging furiously.

And beyond Campbell stood the most beautiful lass Travis had ever seen.

Unfortunately, her lovely features were distorted by an expression of pure terror.

That expression could mean only one thing. The woman was about to scream.

Travis did what he had to do. As her lips formed a shocked "O," he lunged out of the box, seized the back of her head, and clapped his other hand over her mouth.

His actions were utterly ungentlemanly. Brutal. Barbaric.

But they were a necessary evil. Like cauterizing a wound.

Until Travis could figure out what had happened— how he'd gotten here and why he'd been put in a box in the hold of a ship—he was sure that drawing attention to his predicament couldn't be a good thing.

The woman was too stunned for the moment to struggle against him. But that wouldn't last forever.

And though he'd temporarily subdued her, his dog was not so easy to silence.

Campbell began barking. With delight. Or excitement. Or rage. Travis wasn't sure which.

But if he kept it up, the blasted terrier was going to bring the entire ship's crew down on them.

"Campbell!" he hissed. "Be quiet!"

As usual, the stubborn dog ignored him.

"Campbell!" he whispered fiercely.

Still the cursed beast defied him.

From the corner of his eye, Travis saw the lass lowering her mortified gaze.

It was then Travis realized he was bare-chested, dressed in naught but his smallclothes.

And he heard the sound of approaching footsteps.

He acted on instinct.

Releasing the lass, he snatched up Campbell in one hand.

Then, holding the pup strategically in front of his scantily clad *genitalia*, he straightened to face with courage whatever consequences were about to arrive.

If Charlotte weren't still reeling with shock, she might have fallen into a fit of laughter. The man was actually trying to look dignified, despite his obvious dearth of clothing and his hilariously clever attempt to cover that fact. With a dog.

But he'd startled the dickens out of her, springing out of that trunk like a ghoulish Jack-in-the-box.

And when he'd lunged toward her, seizing her head in his hands, her life had flashed before her eyes.

Did he mean to steal her breath? Snap her neck? And drag her to hell?

In the next blink of an eye, she realized three things.

One—he wasn't dead, not even a little.

Two—he didn't intend to hurt her.

And three—he was just as confused as she was.

Four things, she amended. For someone freshly sprung from a coffin, he was about as handsome a corpse as she'd ever seen.

And she was fairly sure—once he'd let her go and whisked up the terrier—he'd have a reasonable explanation for his behavior.

But as the burly chief officer breached the door of the hold, demanding to know what was going on, the Jack-in-the-box was struck speechless.

At the man's lack of an explanation, the chief officer ground out, "We don't abide stowaways on this ship."

Charlotte took one look at the humiliated black terrier and blurted out, "He's not a stowaway, officer. He belongs to me."

She meant to snatch the wee pup away at that point and hold him protectively against her bosom. But she dared not remove him from his current occupation.

Both men turned to her, baffled.

"I meant to keep him in my cabin," she explained.

The chief officer glowered.

"I don't know how he got out," she lied.

The naked man frowned.

"But I assure ye 'twon't happen again," she promised.

The two men were still looking at her with perplexed glares.

She bit her lip. She had to convince them.

"I'll feed him scraps from the table. He won't make a peep, I promise. And at night he can curl up next to—"

The naked man cleared his throat.

The chief officer straightened. "Now see here, Miss..."

Glancing back and forth between the men, she abruptly realized her mistake. The stowaway wasn't the dog. It was the man.

"Oh." Her face grew hot. *"Oh."*

By then, of course, she felt it was too late to withdraw her offer. To do so would have been rude.

Thinking quickly to cover her error, she said, "Once the privacy curtain is installed, o' course." Then, remembering the best defense was a good offense, she turned to the officer, crossly crossing her arms. "Where *is* that curtain anyway?" she demanded. "I requested it hours ago."

While the officer gaped like a trout, Travis had to bite his lip to keep from grinning.

The lass was quick of wit. That was certain. Faced with a humiliating situation, she'd managed to think on her feet and even rock the officer back on his heels.

If only Travis had been able to think that quickly when he'd been caught with Mrs. Wyndham's unmentionables about her ankles, he might not have suffered his current fate.

But he'd been too concerned about the compromised state of Mrs. Wyndham's health to string together a plausible excuse for his presence in her bedroom. Which was how he'd ended up in the ludicrous position of agreeing to duel her husband in order to defend her honor.

Travis realized now that his friends must have drugged him and stowed him on the ship out of desperation, to save him from certain death by dueling pistol.

Still, no matter what the consequences, he had never allowed a woman to bear the brunt of impropriety, even when it meant shouldering blame that didn't belong to him. He wasn't about to start now.

"That won't be necessary, Miss," he said, covering her mistake. "Campbell and I will stay in the hold. When we reach the next port," he told the officer, "I'll disembark. And I'll pay for my passage. I give ye my word."

How he'd do that, he wasn't sure. It appeared his mates had left him neither clothing nor coin. But he had patients in several towns. Surely one of them would be willing to temporarily cover his debt.

"The next port?" the officer groused. *"The next port?"*

"Aye. Where are we bound? London? Southampton?" He hoped it wasn't too far. He hated to inconvenience his patients. And he did intend to return to Edinburgh eventually. He'd somehow make things right with Lord Wyndham, once the man's bluster blew over.

The officer's scowl deepened.

The lass replied with unadulterated cheer, "New York!"

He blinked. "I beg your pardon?" Surely he'd heard wrong.

The officer spoke between clenched teeth. "We're bound for the States."

"The States?" he said in disbelief. "The United States?"

"Some of us are anyway," the officer said in black tones of threat.

Bloody hell! Had his friends actually meant to send him to America? Or had they just stowed him on the next available ship?

The officer narrowed his eyes. "Ye might still be able to swim to Calais if I toss ye overboard now."

"Nay!" the lass cried. "Ye'll do no such thing. I...I meant what I said. Mr. Jameson and his travelin' companion are welcome to stay in my cabin."

Travis was too stunned to realize the lass had called him by name. He was too shaken to even thank her for her mercy.

He couldn't go to America. All his friends were in Edinburgh. Hell, his patients were in Scotland. It could be a year or more by the time he earned enough to pay for return passage.

Maybe he *would* be better off trying to swim for shore.

"If ye'll be so kind as to hang that curtain..." the lass prompted the officer. "We'll also require one o' those sleepin' hammocks. And perhaps ye can send someone to bring him proper clothes."

The officer's scowl deepened as his face purpled. He wasn't accustomed to receiving orders from a woman. If Travis didn't intervene, the lass might end up tossed overboard along with him.

"What if I work for my passage?" he offered. "I've got some doctorin' skills."

"We don't need a doctor," the officer scoffed. "We've got a cook. And he's got a knife."

Travis winced. The state of medicine aboard a ship was appalling. "Then I'll work at whate'er ye need."

"There," the lass decided. "'Tis settled." She arched a brow at the officer and added pointedly, "Unless ye'd rather explain to the captain how a stowaway managed to slip on board...on your watch."

The officer straightened. He knew when he was beaten.

"There's no need to trouble the captain," he grumbled with a slight bow of his head. Then he glared at Travis. He might have capitulated to the lass's request. But that wouldn't stop him from tormenting his new slave of a stowaway at every opportunity. "Ye'll report to me in an hour."

Travis nodded. The officer gave him one last scathing perusal, shook his head, and strode away.

Finally, Travis remembered his manners.

"Thank ye, Miss..."

"Charlotte de Ware."

He blinked. Not the Edinburgh de Wares? Theirs was an old landed family who'd been in Scotland for centuries.

"Pleased to make your acquaintance, Miss de Ware," he said with a respectful dip of his head. "I'm—"

"Mr. Reginald Jameson?" she supplied. At his puzzled frown, she smiled and added, "It says so on your trunk."

Continuing to clutch Campbell against his nether regions, he turned carefully away and returned the half-broken lid to its proper position. There it was in block letters. MR. REGINALD JAMESON. His uncle's name.

Reginald Jameson lived in New York. Which meant Travis's friends had indeed meant to send him to America. They must have known Sir Wyndham would comb every inch of Scotland to find him. And they believed he'd be better off in the hands of his eccentric and enterprising uncle than facing off against a jealous husband. He hoped they were right.

As they stood conversing like casual acquaintances—Charlotte and the mostly naked man before her—it was all she could do to maintain her equilibrium. Not only were her limbs adjusting to the motions of the ship. Her sensibilities were being pulled to and fro by the sight of the handsome stowaway before her.

He was definitely not a gentleman, despite his good manners. His dark hair was longer than was fashionable and unruly. His angular jaw was bristled. And his physique was far from the fleshy, pale ideal of the idle rich. He looked instead like a laborer, trim and fit.

What was it he'd said? That he had some doctoring skills? Glancing at his well-muscled arms, she guessed he wasn't a physician of prestige. He must be a surgeon then. Most surgeons she'd seen were barely a notch above a butcher.

She gulped. The enormity of what she'd offered to this perfect stranger was beginning to sink in.

What would George say? How would he feel, having to share his half of the cabin with a stowaway of questionable character? Not to mention the man's protective mongrel?

Hoping to learn more about her cabin mate, she tried to make light conversation. "So tell me, Mr. Reginald Jameson, how did ye come to stow yourself away on a ship?"

"Travis, Miss," the man said.

"I beg your pardon?"

"My name is *Travis* Jameson. Reginald is my uncle."

"I see."

She didn't see at all. Indeed, she was trying *not* to see. It was difficult to think while her vision was dominated by the sight of a bare-chested, bare-legged man.

"So ye climbed into his trunk and…"

"'Twas not by choice, I assure ye. I believe my friends enclosed me in there—"

"Your friends?" she asked in disbelief. "What kind of friends would impress ye into service?"

It was common for captains of the Royal Navy to drag drunken men aboard their ships and sail away, forcing them to become sailors. She'd never heard of anyone dragging a man aboard a merchant vessel.

"'Tis a complicated tale," he admitted. "But I think they meant well. They intended for me to be delivered into my uncle's safe hands."

His answers only invited more questions. Why hadn't the man's friends simply paid for his passage? Why had they sent him all the way to America? Why had they left Campbell behind, forcing the poor wee dog to leap aboard at the last moment? And why had they left Mr. Jameson in his unmentionables?

Before she could ask any of these questions, a crewman returned with a hammock and a bundle of clothing. The garments were the worst sort—a wrinkled linen shirt and a stained blue jacket, short and sloppy sailor's trousers, threadbare stockings, and a pair of worn leather shoes.

But he seemed glad of any clothing at all.

And Charlotte was glad for an excuse to depart.

"I'll take Campbell to the cabin." She held out her arms for the dog.

But the man held him fast. "I'm grateful for your offer, Miss. Truly I am. But I won't stay in your cabin. 'Twould tarnish your reputation. Campbell and me, we'll be fine here in the hold."

She furrowed her brow. The hold was dark and cold. Even her *Orchidacaea* wouldn't survive six weeks here.

"'Tis a very long journey, sir."

"This will do." By his satisfied expression as he glanced around the hold, one would have thought he was perusing a grand manor house. "I'll hang the hammock here," he said, indicating a pair of beams, "and let the sea rock me gently to sleep."

She had to smile at that. The man was clearly a romantic.

And indeed, part of her was relieved. Convincing George of the merits of showing charity to a common stowaway—not to mention his scruffy companion—would have been a challenge.

"If ye're certain…"

"I am, Miss," he said, inclining his head. "And I thank ye for your kindness."

With a blush and a quick bob, she left.

She took one last tour of the deck, searching for George, to no avail.

By the time she entered her stateroom, the privacy curtain had been hung. It was not very attractive. It hung from the beam, subdividing the cabin like a sail. In fact, it may have *been* a sail.

She lifted the corner to peer in at the other side. Her brother wasn't there.

She supposed it was useless to be cross with him. After all, George would turn up eventually. In the meantime, she'd unpack her trunks and settle in for the journey.

She had filled the armoire with her clothing and just slipped the last of her books onto the captain's already crowded shelves when seven bells were rung for dinner.

The captain set an elegant table, under the circumstances, with porcelain, silver, and crystal. There were ten other privileged guests in all, six single men and two with wives. But they managed to sit comfortably around the great mahogany table that dominated the saloon.

There were introductions, sumptuous food, and frothy conversation. But Charlotte had difficulty enjoying it, since George had conspicuously refused the captain's invitation to dinner. Indeed, she neglected mentioning her brother to anyone, for fear of drawing attention to his unforgivable slight.

At the end of the meal, Charlotte remembered Campbell. She secreted away part of her thick slice of roast pork and a buttered roll in a cloth napkin, which she smuggled into the hold.

Campbell was there by himself, sitting beside the wood trunk. He regarded her with quiet dignity, much like his master, as if to say he was perfectly fine living here in the dim, dank, dark of the hold.

He did perk up, however, when she laid out the feast she'd brought. The starving thing wolfed down the meal with such eagerness, she feared he might eat the napkin.

When she retrieved the napkin and turned to go, Mr. Jameson was just arriving.

Startled to find her there, he nearly dropped his parcel. A napkin full of bread.

"Well, Campbell," she said with a grin, "aren't ye a lucky dog? Now ye'll have *two* dinners."

Mr. Jameson grinned back.

And Charlotte's heart nearly stopped.

He'd washed his face. He'd pulled his overlong hair back into a neat tail. And his broad smile displayed teeth as white as a *Dendrobium crumenatum* orchid.

His clothes might be ragged and rumpled. Too tight in some places. Too loose in others. But he somehow managed to look as distinguished as a duke. And as handsome as a rake.

She'd just opened her mouth to ask him what tasks he'd been set to when the chief officer's voice growled out from the hatch above.

"Mr. Jameson!"

"Aye, sir!" he called back, giving her a sheepish shrug.

She took the rest of the bread for Campbell.

"Go on," she said with a wink. "I'll see his belly is full."

Travis had never worked so hard in his life. The price of stowing away on a vessel was apparently steep.

He spent an hour scrubbing the brass fixtures in the maproom. He stitched ripped sails for another hour. In the galley, he helped cut up vegetables for the crew's evening stew. Then the chief officer sent him topside to swab the deck. By the time the crew gathered at the mess table for their afternoon break, his palms were raw, stinging from the seawater.

The rest of the men were pleasant enough, though a rough lot. They were a motley crew of salt-toughened seadogs and fresh-faced lads, ruddy Scots and dark-skinned foreigners. They offered Travis a tankard of grog and swapped tales of their adventures while docked in Edinburgh.

"What a prime night I had," a Scotsman declared. "There's naught finer than Edinburgh cherry, am I right, lads?"

Several of the men cheered.

"Edinburgh?" an islander scoffed. "Ah, but you have not been to my homeland. I tell you, nothing compares to the ladies of Jamaica."

Most of the men issued friendly boos of protest.

"Wait, lads!" a third chimed in. "Ezra may be right. I've been to Jamaica. And I've ne'er sampled sweeter quim than that of Ezra's ma."

The crew guffawed at that. Even Ezra had to laugh.

One of the younger lads bragged, "I rogered a different doxy every night last week."

"Every night? Is that so?" a stout Highlander replied, adding as an aside to the rest of the crew, "With his wee purse, they must have been three-penny uprights."

Everyone roared with laughter.

A grizzled graybeard barked out, "As long as ye didn't bring the clap back with ye."

A man with ginger-colored hair answered for the lad. "'Tis all right, McGee. The ladies all assured him they were virgins."

More laughter made the rounds.

"Besides," the redhead added, "we've got our own nimgimmer on board now, isn't that right, Doc?" He turned to Travis.

News apparently traveled fast on board a ship. Though Travis wasn't a nimgimmer, the slang for a specialist in venereal disease, he might need to become one if the crew's boasts were at all true.

"Is that right? Have we got us a Sawbones?"

Travis grimaced. He hated that term. He'd stitched up gashes, cauterized wounds, and removed tumors. But he'd not once sawed off a limb. "Aye, I'm a surgeon." And just to be sure the nickname wouldn't stick, he added, "Ye can call me Jameson."

"Wait." The boastful lad's eyes widened. "I know ye. Ye were at The White Hart last night, aye? *Travis* Jameson?"

Travis's hand stiffened on his tankard. He nodded carefully.

"They say ye're a buck o' the first head," the lad marveled, "cuckoldin' half the lords o' Scotland!"

The men looked at him in shocked reverence.

"Is it true?" the redhead asked. "Are ye a fancy man?"

Before he could deny it, the others chimed in.

"A scapegrace."

"And a scoundrel."

"A rascal."

"The worst o' the riff raff."

"He's one of *us,* lads!"

The crew burst out in laughter and clapped Travis on the back. By then, it was too late to change their minds. Like everyone else of his acquaintance, they'd decided he was a philanderer. It seemed pointless to argue with them. And indeed, it served his interests— and the interests of his patients—to let them believe that fiction.

But apparently, the lad had learned more at The White Hart than just about Travis's reputation.

"Ye stowed away 'cause o' the duel, didn't ye?" he cried. He turned to the others, telling the story in excited tones, "One o' the cuckolds challenged Mr. Jameson to pistols at dawn this morn!"

Travis frowned. He was sure he'd be labeled a coward for running away from a duel. A caitiff. And a cur. And that was going to make the rest of the ship's journey even more miserable.

But the sailors lived in a different world. A world where it was more respected to be cunning than brave.

"Clever lad!" one of them said, punching him in the shoulder. "He'll ne'er find ye in America."

"And ye'll get a crack at a whole new bevy o' doves!"

"Here's to the lasses of America!" someone yelled, raising a tankard. "And beware to the poor sods who call them wife!"

Everyone laughed and cheered, taking a swig.

What else could Travis do but lift his tankard and drain it?

CHAPTER 4

Charlotte's cheeks were aflame, and her ears were burning. She knew her habit of listening at doors was wrong. But she convinced herself she was doing important investigation. After all, if Mr. Jameson was truly a scoundrel, she should reconsider her acquaintance with him.

What she heard confirmed her worst fears. Not only was he an unapologetic roué, he was a coward who had run away from a fight. And apparently, he'd lied to her about it. Charlotte could think of nothing more despicable.

Thank heavens, she couldn't decipher much of what the sailors were saying. But she was sure most of it was filthy.

Before she could be subjected to any more disappointing revelations, she turned on her heel and repaired to her stateroom again.

She was quite finished with Mr. Jameson. He'd shown his true colors. She would have naught more to do with him.

Of course, there was still the matter of the man's terrier. She couldn't abandon Campbell. It wasn't right to blame an innocent pup for the sins of his master. So she'd continue to bring him food.

But she vowed she'd not utter another word to Mr. Jameson.

Unfortunately, her promise was tested a few hours later. The chief officer, evidently unaware of Mr. Jameson's scandalous reputation, saw fit to allow the rogue to serve at supper.

Charlotte was already dismayed by the fact she still hadn't located her brother. She wondered if he'd drunk himself into a stupor somewhere. But it was doubly upsetting to have to face the undeniably charming Travis Jameson for the first time since learning of his disgraceful character.

Determined to pay him no heed, she nonetheless found her glance straying to him as he poured Madeira for the diners, offered up a basket of soft rolls, and dished out the salmon-gundy with surprising care and skill.

Once, when the silver-haired matron at the table,

Lady Forbes, addressed Charlotte, she'd been so distracted by the way Mr. Jameson's fingers caressed the stem of her glass as he refilled it that she had to have the question repeated.

"I wondered if this was your first ocean voyage, Miss de Ware," Lady Forbes said.

"Oh. Aye."

Charlotte smiled, and then she couldn't think of anything else to add, creating an awkward silence, at which point the matron turned to the young lady across the table. "And you, Lady Adams?"

Charlotte glanced at Lady Adams.

The woman looked as if she'd seen a ghost. She quickly lowered her gaze and murmured, "I've never seen...never been on an ocean voyage."

Charlotte narrowed her eyes. What was troubling Lady Adams? The young woman's fingers trembled as she reached for her Madeira. She took a generous swallow, as if she meant to steady her nerves.

"Well, 'tis *my* fourth voyage," the elder woman announced, "and I can tell you there's naught to fret about, my dear."

But Charlotte didn't think it was the voyage that worried Lady Adams. And she observed, as the conversation continued blithely on, that the woman's fingers tightened on her glass whenever Mr. Jameson neared the table. Charlotte began to suspect Lady Adams might be acquainted with the stowaway.

Her suspicions were all but confirmed when she glanced up to see Mr. Jameson catching Lady Adams' eye and giving her an almost imperceptible nod.

That gesture could mean only one thing. Mr. Jameson *did* know Lady Adams. And there could be only one way a titled lady and a notorious rake like Travis could have crossed paths.

The nervous Lady Adams must have availed herself of Mr. Jameson's charms. She was upset, clearly afraid the scoundrel would reveal their acquaintance to her husband.

Charlotte, disgusted and perturbed, spared a glance at Lord Adams. He seemed a decent enough fellow and not uncomely. He continued to fork salmon-gundy into his mouth, completely oblivious to the drama unfolding around him.

By the time the sweetened flummery was served to finish the meal, Lady Adams seemed reassured that Mr. Jameson wouldn't expose her secret. She'd even begun to laugh and jest with Lady Forbes.

Charlotte vowed to forget about Mr. Jameson and his licentious indiscretions. She had more pressing concerns, after all. Concerns like visiting Elgin Garden. Keeping her orchids alive. And finding her brother.

She toyed with her flummery, having lost her appetite.

The captain leaned toward her to murmur, "I trust the accommodations are to your likin', Miss?"

"Oh, aye," she said. "Ye've been quite generous, Captain."

"'Tis an honor," he confided, motioning to Mr. Jameson to come refill his glass, "bein' entrusted to see the daughter o' Lord Charles de Ware to America."

She smiled, scraping a spoonful of flummery from her bowl.

Something struck her as odd about his statement. He'd made no mention of George, the *son* of Lord Charles. Was it just an oversight? Or was the captain subtly pointing out George's absence from the table?

"I fear I must apologize on my brother George's behalf," she said as Travis poured the captain's Madeira. "'Tis the most curious thing. But I've not seen him since we left port." She gave a little laugh and slipped the spoon into her mouth. The flummery was sickeningly sweet.

The captain chortled as if she'd made a jest.

She blinked, choking down the bite of flummery.

Then he drew his brows together in puzzlement. "Your brother?"

"Aye," she said. "He went to speak to the chief officer, and I haven't seen him since."

"Your brother," the captain clarified.

At the sound of the captain's consternation, the rest of the diners grew silent.

Humiliated, Charlotte felt the need to explain to everyone. "George is not normally so unsociable. I fear he may feel ill or...or perhaps lost his way on the ship." She didn't want to say what she really feared—that he'd gone off to someone's cabin and gambled away his coin or lost himself at the bottom of a tankard of grog.

"But, Miss," the captain said gently, "he's not on the ship. He only purchased passage for one."

Charlotte froze. What was he talking about? Of course George was on the ship. The captain must be mistaken.

And yet even as she had that thought, she realized it could be true.

George had been acting strange all morn, quiet and out of sorts.

He'd never returned to the stateroom.

He'd never moved the settee.

He'd never hung the curtain.

Perhaps he'd never even made the request to the chief officer.

All at once, she couldn't speak. Couldn't breathe. The flummery she'd just swallowed sank like a stone. Fear coiled in her belly. The faces around the table swam before her eyes.

Was it true? Had George bought only one ticket?

Was she alone?

All by herself in the midst of the vast, roiling ocean?

Abandoned and cast adrift on unfamiliar seas?

Suddenly she felt sick. The blood left her face. Sweat broke out on her brow. And she felt her stomach lurch in rebellion.

"Come with me," Mr. Jameson said sharply, banging the bottle down on the table as he seized Charlotte by the elbow.

If she'd had a shred of strength left in her, she would have resisted. But he would brook no argument. While everyone at the table gasped at the liberties he was taking, he scraped back her chair and hauled her to her feet.

"Here now!" the captain protested.

"She's ill," Travis called over his shoulder.

He half-dragged, half-carried her up the stairs to the weather deck, where the cold, fresh air felt like a slap across her face. She still felt nauseated, but at least the immediate urge to empty her stomach was gone.

"There," he said, securing her hands on the railing. "Better?"

She nodded.

She only felt better by degrees. But at least she didn't feel as if her knees might buckle beneath her.

"Keep your eyes on the horizon," he directed. "'Twill help ye keep your bearin's."

Charlotte stared out across the indigo water. At the flecks of white foam that floated atop the waves. And the orange-hued clouds that clung to the horizon below the darkening twilight sky.

She wasn't sure she would ever regain her bearings.

What had happened? What had George done? Why had he sent her off alone on this ship?

She shivered as the wind teased the bottle green silk of her gown.

Mr. Jameson quickly tore off his jacket. Not satisfied to simply hand her the garment, he placed it upon her shoulders, then turned her toward him to straighten the jacket and fasten the top button.

"Thank ye," she whispered, grateful for the warmth of the garment enveloping her.

It was shocking how quickly she'd been reduced to seeking refuge in the arms of the very scapegrace she'd hoped to avoid.

Yet his eyes as he gazed down at her were full of genuine empathy and concern.

Suddenly it felt like this man she'd barely met was her only friend in the world.

It was no wonder, she thought, the handsome rake was able to talk so many lasses out of their unmentionables.

Travis regretted having to strong-arm Miss de Ware to the weather deck. But he knew if he'd waited one more instant, the poor lass would have cast up her accounts all across the captain's dining table.

Sometimes, when attempting an unpleasant but necessary task, like setting a bone or removing a splinter, expeditiousness was best.

He was just as relieved for the breath of fresh air anyway. Seeing one of his former patients on the arm of her husband in the intimate quarters of the saloon had unsettled him. He wondered if he'd leaped from the frying pan into the fire. On board a ship, there was no escaping a jealous spouse.

Her anxious manner certainly didn't help things. She looked like she might blurt out a damning confession at any moment.

Fortunately, he was able to catch her eye and give her a nod to assure her of his discretion. He meant to feign ignorance. No secret would be spilled from his lips. As far as anyone knew, they had never met.

Lady Adams seemed to trust him after that. He felt he could be certain of her silence on the matter.

As far as his current patient, Miss de Ware would be easier to cure than Lady Adams had been. She was suffering from shock and seasickness. Lingering on deck a while would cure her seasickness. As for her shock...

"Why?" she asked, gazing up at him with eyes as wide and blue as the evening sea. "Why would George send me alone to America?"

Why indeed? He couldn't say. In his view, a man would have to be mad to abandon his sister among the sort of riff raff that inhabited a packet ship.

He might not be able to solve her predicament. But he could bloody well offer her his protection.

"That I don't know, Miss. But ye've no cause for worry. I'll watch o'er ye. 'Tis the least I can do to repay ye for your kindness." He placed reassuring palms lightly on her shoulders. "Ye have my word. I vow I'll defend ye and see ye safely to port."

"Ye will?" Despite her dire situation, she lifted a brow, and an involuntary giggle erupted from her, startling him. "And who will defend me from *ye?*"

Her remark set him back on his heels. He released her like a hot coal. "What do ye mean?"

She seemed to regret her accusation almost at once. "I'm sorry, Mr. Jameson. 'Tis a kind offer. But I fear your reputation as a villain precedes ye."

He frowned. She'd known him less than a day. How could she already have formed an opinion about him?

Then he remembered the crew. Perhaps one of the loose-lipped sailors had warned Miss de Ware about trafficking with a scoundrel like him.

"I must protest, Miss de Ware. I assure ye my reputation is largely unfounded."

"Is it?"

Her eyes dipped to his mouth, as if judging whether lies fell from his lips. Then, though he was sure she wasn't aware of it, she wet her lips with the tip of her tongue.

If she'd known how inviting a gesture that was, she never would have made it. Especially not toward a man she considered a villain.

But something about the way she was staring at his mouth and the languid drift of her gaze back up to his eyes made him see her—not as a patient and not as an innocent he'd just vowed to protect—but as a woman.

A beautiful woman.

A desirable woman.

For the first time in his life, he almost wished he *were* a rake. In that moment, with the sea breeze gently blowing her dark curls, her dreamy eyes fixed on his, her delicate shoulders dwarfed beneath the oversized sailor's coat, he wanted naught more than to plant a long, lingering kiss on her alluring mouth.

"A Christmas gift," she murmured.

"I beg your pardon?" For one mad moment, Travis thought she might have read his mind.

"George said 'twas like a Christmas gift, goin' to New York."

Travis frowned. It appeared they *would* arrive just before Christmas. "Aye?"

"Maybe he couldn't afford the passage for two," she said hopefully. "Maybe he was too ashamed to tell me." She tucked the corner of her tempting lip under her teeth. "He knew how much I wanted to see Elgin."

"Elgin?" he said, surprised at the way his heart fell. He suddenly wondered if she would let Elgin kiss that bonnie mouth.

"George promised me we'd go."

"And will this Elgin watch o'er ye once ye're in New York?" Travis might never avail himself of her charms. But he was still concerned for her welfare.

"What?" She was gaping at him in confusion.

"Is he an honorable gentleman?"

"Who?"

"Elgin."

For the first time since they'd left the captain's table, Charlotte's face dissolved into a grin of genuine amusement. "Not who. What. Elgin Botanic Garden."

His brows came together. He knew that name.

"David Hosack's garden?" he asked.

She gasped in wonder. "Ye know it?"

"I've heard of it." Every medical student he knew aspired to be like David Hosack. A physician, a professor of natural history, and an expert botanist, Hosack had famously treated the American statesman Alexander Hamilton after his fatal duel. With Elgin Botanic Garden, Hosack was helping to determine the usefulness of native plants, contributing to the field of medicine.

"George promised to take me there," she said, her eyes alight. Then, as if a cloud passed across her face, they dimmed. She realized her brother's promises were empty now.

"I'll take ye to Elgin," he blurted out.

"What?"

He shrugged. "Why not? 'Twould be of interest to me as well."

"'Twould?"

He nodded.

If he'd stopped to think for one instant, he would never have made such a rash promise. The lass was not his responsibility. She probably didn't even want to be seen with a man of his questionable virtue. Besides, Travis had much bigger problems of his own to solve. He also didn't have a pence to his name.

But he couldn't bear to see the disappointment in her face.

Surgeons were supposed to fix people, damn it.

And Miss de Ware desperately needed his help.

"I'd consider it an honor," he told her.

She rewarded him with a bright smile and a soft cry of glee. And when she impulsively reached for his hand, clasping it gratefully between her own, he hardly noticed the pain as she squeezed the rubbed-raw flesh of his palm.

It was a failing of Charlotte's—in addition to her reckless sense of curiosity—that she was prone to acting on impulse.

She should never have accepted Mr. Jameson's offer of accompanying her to the garden. But once her dreams of going to Elgin seemed crushed, all she'd seen was a dashing hero offering to come to her rescue. So relieved and delighted was she by his gesture that she completely forgot about his past.

His scandalous reputation.

His sinfully wanton behavior.

His adulterous dalliances.

And now she'd put herself in the position of holding his hand.

Not that it was unpleasant. His flesh was warm, and there was a nimble strength in his fingers. But now that she'd clasped his hand, she wasn't sure how to gracefully *un*clasp it.

One side of his mouth curved up in a smile. His eyes sparkled like dark crystals. A tendril of his chestnut hair had come loose and hung with rakish charm over his brow. Merciful heavens. The man was as handsome as Lucifer himself.

'Twas little wonder his affections were in demand.

But of course, she wouldn't hold him to his promise. Once they reached New York, she'd release him from his obligation, which he'd obviously made in haste. She was sure her mother's cousin Eugenia would be glad to accompany her to the garden.

Meanwhile, she shouldn't remain in the company of such a man. She should stop staring into those

glittering, dangerous eyes. And she absolutely must release his hand.

She told herself she would.

In another moment.

When a convenient opportunity arose.

"Ahoy!" one of the crewmen shouted. "What's goin' on there?"

Charlotte gasped. But Mr. Jameson gently extracted his hand and took a smooth step backward, salvaging her honor.

"Miss de Ware required a bit o' fresh air," he called back. "I'm makin' certain she doesn't tumble overboard."

The watchman waved to acknowledge his reply and turned away.

"Thank ye," Charlotte whispered, glad he'd made excuses for her.

He gave her a polite nod.

Then she smirked. A man like Mr. Jameson was probably accustomed to such subterfuge. He was likely an expert at slipping out of a lady's embrace and climbing out of a mistress's window.

"Do ye feel well enough to return to the saloon?" he asked.

She furrowed her brow. "Oh, I couldn't." She didn't think she could endure the double humiliation. First, her confusion regarding her brother. And second, having left the table so abruptly.

"I can take a quick peek and see if they've finished," he offered.

"Would ye?"

"Wait here a moment. And hold fast to the railin'."

Charlotte did cling to the railing, but not because she feared tumbling overboard. Her heart was racing, and she felt dizzy from her encounter with the charming Mr. Jameson.

The evening sky had now turned a deep purple, as dark as the markings on an *Oncidium pulchellum.* But unlike the flower's markings, which directed insects to the pollen-covered stamen, the cloud-covered heavens offered no direction.

Charlotte too felt as if she traveled under a starless sky, without guidance or direction. Would George have been so willing to send her off alone if he'd known in whose hands she'd end up?

Surely not, she decided. Yet a part of her was almost glad George wasn't on board. It might be wicked and reckless of her, but she was rather glad of Mr. Jameson's company.

He returned after a moment. "'Tis all clear," he said with a wink.

"Oh!" She suddenly remembered the wee stowaway. "I forgot to save some salmon-gundy for Campbell."

"I'll give him a bite o' my dinner."

"Ye haven't dined yet?"

"Nay, the crew eats after the officers."

"That hardly seems fair. The crew labors twice as hard as the officers."

"True enough. But sometimes," he confided with a lift of his brow, "life isn't fair."

She realized then how selfish she'd been, blubbering because her brother had sent her to New York on her own. At least she had a seat at the captain's table. And family with whom to spend Christmas in New York. And return passage to Scotland.

Poor Mr. Jameson had been stowed away against his wishes. He was forced to do hard labor lest he be tossed overboard. And he'd arrive in America with nary a cent.

"Shall we?" he said, offering his arm.

For a roué, he had very good manners. He helped her down the steps and accompanied her to her stateroom.

Then, in typical physician fashion, he lowered his brows and advised, "If ye feel a twinge o' seasickness again, ring for an officer to prop open your windows. The fresh air should settle your constitution."

"Aye, sir," she said with a smile, giving him a mock salute.

He grinned back and gave her a slight bow.

She had just entered the stateroom and closed the door behind her when she remembered his coat. She swiftly opened the door again.

"Pssst!" she hissed, "Mr. Jameson!"

He turned.

"Ye forgot your coat."

She'd begun to unbutton the garment when she saw his eyes widen. She blushed, realizing what she'd said and what it looked like. Without a word, he strode quickly to the cabin. She swiftly removed the coat and handed it over.

A trace of a grin touched his lips as he shook his head and left with prudent haste.

Securing the door behind her, she leaned back against it, sighing at her foolishness. Hopefully, no one had witnessed their exchange. If being in the company of the scandalous Mr. Jameson hadn't already ruined her reputation, she might just manage to do it herself.

CHAPTER 5

Eight bells had sounded when Charlotte blew out the candle in her stateroom and climbed under the covers of the large feather bed. Lying in the dark, peering out the window at the endless black ocean, she felt vulnerable and insignificant.

She'd been uprooted from her comfortable home. Enclosed in a wee, dark, wooden box. And sent on a journey to a strange new world.

Just like her orchids.

She couldn't be sure whether either of them would flounder or thrive. She had to try as best she could—for her flowers and herself—to maintain a semblance of order, a sense of normalcy.

Mr. Jameson was threatening that. He was not a normal part of her life at all. Like the waves rocking

the ship, his presence left her unsteady and off-kilter. He was unpredictable, dangerous, and distracting. A man like him could make her forget her priorities and neglect her duties. He could make her forget who she was.

And yet there was something exhilarating about being in his presence. Something life-giving. And attracting. An energy emanated from him, as potent as the buzzing of a bee, tempting the tightly closed bud of her sheltered heart to blossom.

She exhaled into her pillow, unsure whether it was a sigh of dread or relief. If she wished to survive this journey, she would have to confront her inexplicable attraction to Mr. Jameson and decide whether he was a companion plant or a parasite.

As it turned out in the end, she needn't have worried so much. She actually didn't encounter Mr. Jameson much in the daily schedule she set for herself.

Her botany studies kept her busy in her stateroom most morns. The trunk George had brought aboard—the trunk he claimed contained his clothes—he'd thoughtfully filled instead with her books. So there was plenty to keep her entertained.

She left the orchid boxes open during the day to let the leaves soak up the southern sunlight. She took detailed notes and measurements, observing that the plants seemed to have gone into a sort of growth stasis. A few blooms dropped off, which was not unexpected, considering the shock they'd undergone.

She always stopped by the hold at midday to give Campbell a good scratching and to bring him a wee bite of dinner. But Mr. Jameson was never there. She supposed the chief officer kept him busy elsewhere on the ship.

On rainy days, she remained in her cabin, reading or sketching. She'd started making her own illustrations of her orchids, diagramming the various parts according to Linnaeus's designations. It was a challenging task, considering the variations in the flowers. In some, the *rostellum* was nearly impossible to locate, deep within the flower. In others, the size differential between the lateral *sepal* and the *labellum* was so minor as to be indistinguishable.

On sunny afternoons, she strolled above deck, enjoying the temperate breeze ruffling her muslin skirts and wafting through her curls. She squinted up at the sapphire blue skies across which stout ships of white cloud sometimes sailed. She gazed down at dark teal waves tipped with pale foam.

Still, she rarely encountered Mr. Jameson. Whatever deck she occupied, he was assigned work elsewhere. It seemed almost as if the captain and chief officer conspired to keep them apart.

Perhaps that was for the best. After all, once they arrived in New York, they would likely never see each other again.

She'd decided unequivocally that she would release Mr. Jameson from his promise to take her to Elgin. Coming to terms with the fact she was alone on this journey, she was determined to buck up and face her fate with courage.

She learned to bathe in a small tub of lukewarm rainwater. To fall asleep in the cradle of the sea. To use a bucket of ocean water for a chamberpot. Even to enjoy a tankard of grog.

There was no reason she couldn't employ this newfound independence to find her own way to Elgin.

It wasn't until a fortnight into the voyage that she found her resolve tested, when the chief officer assigned Mr. Jameson to the saloon again to serve supper. Apparently, it was an assignment not to the chief officer's liking. He despised the stowaway and made no bones about saying so. But the regular server was suffering from some illness, and no other crewman possessed the finesse to serve the captain's refined guests.

When she entered the saloon and saw Mr. Jameson standing with his hands formally clasped behind him, she felt her heart leap unexpectedly. She beamed at him. He winked at her. And then she remembered her place and the other diners. The chief officer gave her a scowl, and she glanced away, making her giddy way to the table.

She'd forgotten just how attractive Travis Jameson was. How his mahogany eyes twinkled. How that lock

of dark hair fell with lusty allure over his brow. How his lips curved at the corners with sly humor.

But seeing him now, she would have sworn he was even more handsome than before. A fortnight spent in the warmth of the sun and the invigorating spray of the ocean, hauling rope and swabbing decks, had weathered his fair skin and toughened his muscles. He looked vibrant and refreshed. Ignoring him proved to be a Herculean task.

She hardly tasted her food. She barely recalled what was served. And she almost forgot to save a bite for Campbell.

After supper, Lady Adams, the woman with the questionable past with Mr. Jameson, delayed Charlotte's departure, requesting a word with her in private. What she could want, Charlotte didn't know. She hoped Lady Adams wasn't going to launch into some sort of jealous tirade. Charlotte might enjoy the friendship of the stowaway. But she certainly had no designs upon him. Who would be foolish enough to encourage a liaison with a roué like Mr. Jameson?

Lady Adams would, she decided. Even with a husband of her own. She'd struck up some sort of relationship with the infamous rake. It followed that she might attempt to warn Charlotte away from a man she perceived as her property.

Nonetheless, there was no way to politely refuse the woman. Secreting the napkin full of Campbell's food among her skirts, Charlotte obliged Lady Adams, inviting her into her stateroom.

The lady gazed around the cabin in wonder, exclaiming at the elegance of the furnishings, puzzled by the dividing curtain that Charlotte hadn't bothered to have removed, eyeing with curiosity the books, notes, and botanist tools scattered atop the hastily made bed.

"'Tis a lovely cabin," she said softly.

Charlotte smiled, unsure what to say. She was eager for the lady to get on with whatever stern warning she wished to issue so she could take Campbell his dinner.

"May I?" Lady Adams inquired, indicating the chair.

"Please." Charlotte's shoulders sank as she surrendered the napkin to a table and sat across from Lady Adams. Apparently, the conversation was going to last long enough to warrant chairs.

"If I may be so bold as to inquire," the woman said in a voice that was anything but bold, "how long have ye known Mr. Jameson?"

"Mr. Jameson?" It was as she feared. They were going to discuss Travis. "Not long at all. I met him on the ship."

Lady Adams gave her a sympathetic, disbelieving smile. Then she leaned forward in confidence. "Oh, Miss, ye don't have to conceal anythin' from me. Ye see, I believe we may have somethin' in common."

Charlotte's mouth fell open. Now she truly didn't know what to say. If Lady Adams was referring to her adulterous relationship with Mr. Jameson, they had absolutely nothing in common.

"'Tis naught to be ashamed of," Lady Adams said sweetly.

Charlotte could only stare at the woman. Naught to be ashamed of? She wondered what *Lord* Adams would have to say about that.

"'Tis the very thing Mr. Jameson has been determined to prove," Lady Adams said.

Charlotte's jaw tightened. It was, was it? 'Twas a challenging theory, she supposed, to prove there was naught wrong with adultery.

By Perdition, she was beginning to despise Mr. Jameson. He'd obviously pulled the wool over this naïve woman's eyes. As for Charlotte, he wouldn't find her so easy to gull.

Lady Adams continued. "I just wish to give ye my best wishes, Miss. What he did for me was nothin' short of a miracle. I'm sure he'll do the same for ye."

Charlotte was stunned speechless. She felt her cheeks turn rosy at the lady's frank speech.

Then Lady Adams pressed tentative fingertips to Charlotte's forearm. "Most of all, I want to assure ye, ye need not worry for your reputation. Mr. Jameson is completely trustworthy and thoroughly discreet."

"How nice," Charlotte said, smiling through clenched teeth.

If he was so discreet, then how had Charlotte figured out their relationship long before Lady Adams' confession?

"Well," Lady Adams said, at a loss as to what more she could offer in the way of conversation, "thank ye for your hospitality." She rose, prompting Charlotte to rise as well, and gazed meaningfully into Charlotte's eyes. "Good luck with...with Mr. Jameson and...and..." She gestured to the array of botany materials, which were clearly beyond her understanding. "Your...pursuits."

Once she was finally gone, Charlotte snatched up the napkin of food and stomped out toward the hold, infuriated with the vile Travis Jameson and ready to give him the sharp side of her tongue.

But when she arrived, Campbell was by himself. He perked up when she came in with his food and began madly wagging his tail.

"Here ye go, lad," she said, crouching down to scratch him behind the ear. "Ye're a good pup, aren't ye? Nothin' like your villainous master." She hand-fed him a bite of roast chicken. "Ye'd ne'er lead a lady astray." He wolfed it down, and she gave him another. "Or cuckold a woman's husband." He made quick work of that bite as well, and she placed the next on the flat of her palm. "And then try to claim 'tis naught to be ashamed of." He slurped up the bite, tickling her palm with his tongue.

Then she had to laugh at herself. Campbell was a dog. They weren't the most discriminating of creatures. The wee black terrier would likely mate with any bonnie pup that crossed his path and see naught wrong with it.

It seemed Mr. Jameson *did* have something in common with Campbell after all. They were both dogs. And Charlotte couldn't decide which of them had less scruples.

For days the chief officer had kept Travis busy— repairing rope, polishing brass, cleaning portholes, and endlessly swabbing the deck with seawater to keep the boards from mildewing.

When Travis wasn't doing menial chores, he did minor surgeries. He'd removed a splinter from a young lad's thumb and clipped a fish hook out of a crewman's forearm. He'd suggested an extra serving of ginger-bread to Lord Adams, who tended to feel queasy when the seas got rough. He'd even recommended the chief officer use goose fat as a salve for his blistered heel.

Campbell had fared well enough in the hold, being a good sport and pretending to enjoy his daily ration of lobscouse and hardtack.

But after a fortnight, Travis was convinced he could rule out ship's mate from his list of possible occupations. His complexion had grown unfashionably swarthy from long days spent in the sun. His muscles, which had protested at first, had finally given up the fight, and he could keep up with any of the seasoned crew. His palms were callused, and his fingers were stiff from hauling rope. Like it or not, he was becoming a seaworthy laborer who no longer possessed the refined and sensitive hands of a physician.

His shipmates were good enough company, with a talent for spinning yarns, but they lacked the intellect of his fellow surgeons. He missed conversation about the latest surgical techniques, the development of tumor removal, and notes from the lectures at the University of Edinburgh.

Worse, the crew was unable to let go of the notion that Travis was a "buck of the first head," the most wicked of rogues. So they nagged him for tales of his great exploits. As always, he claimed he was not one to kiss and tell, leaving them to wonder how unspeakably vile his acts of debauchery must be.

It didn't escape his notice that after the watchman had discovered Travis lending assistance to Miss de Ware on the weather deck, the chief officer had made sure that opportunity didn't arise again.

He couldn't blame the man. With the way the crew had painted Travis, he was not the sort of man with which a proper young lady should fraternize.

Still, it staggered the imagination how few times he

even glimpsed the lovely Miss Charlotte. The ship wasn't that big.

So it was a surprise when, after seventeen days at sea, Travis was finally granted an opportunity to see her.

The crewman who normally served at supper had had a severe flare-up of gout, for which Travis prescribed rest and staying away from sweetened rum. It then fell to Travis to serve the meal.

He had to admit it was a relief to trade his bucket of seawater for a bottle of Madeira, even if he wasn't allowed to drink it himself. He could at last be reminded of the civilized man he'd once been and brush up on his gentler manners. He could also steal glances at the lovely Miss de Ware at supper.

She seemed to be blossoming in the fresh sea air.

Unlike some of the passengers the crew referred to as "live lumber," who claimed to be hopelessly bored by the long voyage, despairing of ever touching land again, she took to the ocean like she'd been born to it. He heard her mention her seafaring grandfather at dinner, so perhaps it was true.

And though she never addressed Travis directly, all evening she'd given him secret smiles that set his heart racing.

Too soon, supper was over. By the time Travis finished clearing the table and washing the dishes, the diners had already retired to their staterooms.

Someone had left a piece of roast chicken on their plate, so he'd stolen the morsel for Campbell. The lucky dog would eat well tonight, better than Travis.

The rest of the crew would be gathering soon for their own dinner. Travis decided to feed Campbell before he joined them for their ubiquitous lobscouse.

When he threw open the door of the hold, he was so startled to see an intruder in what he'd grown accustomed to think of as his quarters that he almost dropped Campbell's treat.

Then he saw who it was.

"Miss de Ware," he said with pleasure.

She seemed just as startled as he was. At first. Then she shot to her feet with a frown and demanded, "What are *ye* doin' here?"

Taken aback by her hostile tone, he answered, "I...live here."

Realizing she was the intruder, she nonetheless lifted her chin to say, "I was just bringin' Campbell his dinner. I'll be goin' now."

He didn't want her to leave. He'd forgotten how much he enjoyed her company. Even when she was in a high dudgeon, as she seemed to be now.

"I'm sure Campbell's glad of a visitor. He likes ye, ye know."

She was flustered by his compliment and passed it off with a shrug. "He only likes me because I give him what he wants."

He grinned. "Dogs are not so different from humans, I suspect."

Her eyes went wide with astonishment and outrage. "I don't know what ye mean. I have nothin' ye want."

He would beg to differ with her. She seemed to possess a lot of what he admired in a lass. A kind nature. A brilliant mind. An indomitable spirit.

"I only mean that we're all creatures driven by our desires," he clarified.

That seemed to make her even more livid. "I assure ye, Mr. Jameson, I am *not* driven by my desires." She lowered her voice to a hiss to add, "Ye will not make a wanton of me as ye did Mrs. Adams."

He recoiled in shock. "What?"

Even she seemed to sense she'd overstepped the bounds of politeness. She clapped a hand over her mouth.

"What about Mrs. Adams?" he demanded, narrowing his eyes. He wouldn't let anyone slander a lady's character. Not even Miss Charlotte de Ware.

"I'll say no more," she declared, snatching up her skirts to elbow her way past him.

He stopped her, seizing her arm.

She gasped. "Unhand me, villain!"

"I won't let ye drag a good woman's name through the mud," he said.

"Oh aye," she bit out, trying to tug free, "because what happened between ye is naught to be ashamed of, right?"

He frowned. That was true. "Right."

"Let go o' me!" she barked.

He had no choice then but to do as she asked.

"Ye're despicable," she seethed, sidling past.

That hurt and enraged him. He turned on her with all the force of his frustration.

"I'm despicable? Is that so?" He shook his head. He was anything but despicable.

"I've heard the tales," she fired back. "I know all about ye."

"Indeed? And what have ye heard?"

"That ye're a scoundrel and a rake. A scapegrace and a ne'er-do-well. A rogue and a rascal. A churl and a rake."

"Ye said that already."

"What?"

"A rake. Ye said that already."

"Ye're *twice* a rake."

"Is that so? And what proof do ye have?"

"I've heard it with my own ears."

He clucked his tongue in disappointment. "And I thought ye had more between those ears than stuffin'."

She gasped at the insult. Her mouth formed a great "O" for outrage. Then she clamped her lips in an angry line and closed her eyes to smoldering slits.

When she lost the capacity for words, she gave him a punitive shove. Her actions made Campbell join in the argument, barking in protest as his two best friends in the world sulked in silent but powerful fury.

"If that's how ye feel," he snarled, "then I won't trouble ye with my presence again."

"Fine."

"Fine."

Out of ammunition, Travis fired what he considered a final, futile shot across the bow. "And ye needn't come to the hold again. I'll be feedin' Campbell from now on."

For one instant, she looked hurt. But she recovered quickly with a threat. "Ye know, he probably won't touch the bilge rat stew ye've been eatin'."

"Better that than the hummin'bird's tongues ye've been feedin' him."

They were both too proud to take back their impetuous words.

She growled once, and then bit out, "Good night, sir."

She slammed the door with great force as she exited, making the candle in the hold's lantern gutter out. And Travis was left in the dark with Campbell, whose morose whimpers echoed the hollow pulse of his own sad heart.

It had taken Charlotte half the night to fall asleep. She'd tossed and turned in the soft feather mattress as if it were a bed of nails. Finally she'd managed to stop thinking about the despicable Mr. Jameson when she closed her eyes.

But she woke in an instant when some great force tossed her out of the bed and onto the rug. When she shook the stars from her head and tried to rise, the cabin reeled sideways, and she tumbled onto the wooden planks.

Wind screamed through the gaps of the windows like a keening widow. The books slid off the shelves, dropping onto the deck with a banging like cannonballs. Outside her door, she heard men shouting.

What was happening?

As if gravity had taken a holiday, the furniture shifted, slamming into the bulkheads, first one way, then the other.

Fighting paralyzing fear, Charlotte crawled across the sloping floor and battled her way toward the door.

The chaos was no better when she managed to open the door of the cabin. The lanterns in the saloon swayed wildly, sending jagged shadows across the deckhead and illuminating the panicked faces of the other passengers.

Her heart seized. She wondered if *The Fortuity* was capsizing.

The captain scrambled down the steps to their deck. His face was stern, and his hair was windblown.

"Hold fast!" he cried. "'Tis a nor'easter! Keep to your cabins! We're goin' to batten down the hatches and ride her out!"

With that, he climbed back up, closing and sealing the passage with an iron grate and a tarpaulin. But instead of making Charlotte feel safe, she felt as if she'd been enclosed in a coffin. She was sure the ship would either be blown apart or knocked keel-side-up. And she would end up at the bottom of the sea.

The passengers dutifully followed the captain's orders, staggering back to their cabins and securing the doors.

As for the crew, they were likely battling the storm from the weather deck, striking the sails and heading into the wind. It seemed a perilous place where one stray gale or rogue wave could sweep a man off the deck to his death.

She chewed at her lip.

Mr. Jameson was probably out there.

Which meant Campbell was alone in the hold.

There were trunks and barrels in the hold, butts and crates that could harm a wee terrier. Besides, the poor pup must be terrified.

Ignoring the warnings of the other passengers, she closed her cabin door behind her and zigzagged across the saloon. At some point, she'd ripped her lawn chemise, and it slipped off of her shoulder as she clung to whatever solid handholds she could find. In the passage leading to the hold, she banged her hip on the bulkhead when the ship rocked violently sideways. But somehow she dragged herself to the hold door, tearing her thumbnail on the brass latch as she lugged the door open.

Two frightened eyes shone out at her as Campbell cowered beside Travis's trunk. By some miracle, the lantern was still alight. But as she feared, the contents of the hold were a mess. Crates had come loose from their ropes, and a heavy barrel strained at its tether, tipping and threatening to break free. Parcels hanging on hooks from the deckhead swung like cathedral bells.

"'Tis all right, Campbell!" she shouted. "That's a good lad. Stay there."

But just as she took a step toward him, the ship hit a particularly rough trough, dropping with a sharp and sudden jerk. The deck disappeared abruptly under her feet, sending her tripping across the hold. Her ankle twisted, and a jagged agony coursed like hot lightning up her leg.

Campbell gave a loud yelp of pain.

Ignoring her injury, she clawed her way toward him.

When she reached the pup, he licked her hands and tried to get up. But his back legs were trapped under a wooden crate that had fallen onto its side.

While the wind roared and the wood of the ship creaked a dire warning, Charlotte gritted her teeth against the throbbing in her ankle as she found her footing. She slipped her fingers under the edge of the crate and lifted it up with all her might.

It shifted a few inches, just enough for Campbell to crawl free. Then, as she let the crate slam back down on the deck, the ship wrenched sideways again.

The last thing she saw was a lantern swinging toward her head.

CHAPTER 6

Travis had carved bullets from soldiers injured in battle. He'd removed goiters from sickly noblemen. He'd once sewn up a seven-inch slash made by a gentleman's sword. And he'd set bones broken in carriage accidents.

But naught had unnerved him more than breaking into the hold after the storm and lifting his lantern to find Campbell standing vigil over Miss de Ware. She lay pale and silent on the deck, surrounded by a sea of splintered wood and shattered glass, A trickle of blood marred her brow.

His heart dropped into his stomach. Despair threatened to paralyze his limbs.

But he shoved his emotions down. There was no time for them. He had to think like a physician.

Disregarding his own safety, he knelt beside her in the debris, planting the lantern on the deck by her bare shoulder.

He pressed his fingers against her throat, cursing the calluses that had lessened the sensitivity of his fingertips. Her skin felt clammy. But she had a strong pulse.

He bent down to her, lowering his cheek toward her parted lips. She was still breathing.

Then he lifted her curls carefully away from the gash in her forehead. The cut looked minor, and the blood had clotted. But the knot there indicated a heavy impact. That was probably what had knocked her unconscious.

He needed to rouse her. Current practice suggested that concussion could be prevented by keeping the patient awake.

First, however, he had to make sure there were no other injuries.

Starting at the midline of her skull, he felt for cracks or swelling, moving his fingers outward, and carefully lifting her head to examine the back side. There was a knot there too, where she had hit the deck. But it was dry. The skin hadn't been broken.

He felt the vertebrae at the back of her neck. They seemed in place.

Her clavicle was intact. He swiftly examined each arm from shoulder to wrist—*humerus, ulna, radius*—but found no breaks or swelling.

He ran his fingers gingerly along each of her ribs, a simple task through the thin lawn of her chemise. They appeared to be unharmed.

He flipped her chemise up with brusque efficiency to check her lower limbs. Cradling her left heel in one hand, he gently lifted her leg. The flesh was bruised. But the *femur, patella, tibia,* and *fibula* appeared straight.

Lowering her limb, he moved to her right leg. He saw the injury at once. Her ankle was swollen. There was no way to tell if it was broken until she was conscious.

He covered her limbs against for modesty and slipped her torn chemise back up over her shoulder. He'd learned long ago that the flailing a person did to conceal their body during an examination caused more harm than good.

Then he lightly patted her cheek.

"Miss de Ware," he called softly.

Her eyes twitched.

"Miss de Ware, wake up."

She furrowed her brow.

"Wake up, Miss de Ware."

She gasped in a quick breath, and she blinked. "Campbell!"

To his surprise, the dog woofed back.

Before he could caution Miss de Ware against sudden movement, she pushed up to her elbows, muttering to herself, "Campbell. Campbell's hurt."

Travis frowned. *Was* he? Before he could glance at the dog, she continued rattling on.

"Oh!" she exclaimed. "Mr. Jameson. What happened?" She pressed fingertips to her head, glancing at the blood on her fingers with minimal concern. "Has the storm passed? Are we safe? Where's Campbell? A crate fell on him and—" She tried to get up.

"Miss de Ware!" he interrupted, clutching her shoulder. "Ye've been injured."

"I'm fine," she insisted. "But poor Campbell..."

Travis supposed he wasn't going to get any cooperation from Miss de Ware until he looked after the terrier.

"Promise me ye'll stay put," he said, "and I'll see to Campbell."

"But I'm fine."

He pinched the hem of her chemise between his fingers. Sometimes a single action could say more than a mouthful of words. He flipped back the bottom of her gown, just enough to expose her ankle. "Ye're not fine."

She caught her breath, and her brows rose. "Oh."

"But if ye insist I look after the dog first..."

"I do," she said as he covered her ankle again. "A crate fell on him."

He smirked. The selfless lass cared more about a tough old terrier than she did herself.

"Can ye fix him?" she asked, worry wrinkling her brow.

"Let's see."

Campbell *was* injured. Though the dog put on a brave face, his back leg had been damaged. The skin hadn't been punctured, but the leg was swollen, probably cracked. Travis wasn't sure it could be repaired.

"Is it broken?" she asked.

"Aye."

"But ye can make it better, aye?"

"'Tisn't the same thing, treatin' a dog and a human."

"But ye can do it?"

He hated to dash her hopes. "If 'tis a simple break, perhaps. I can immobilize the limb to let it heal and hope for the best."

"Good." Then, in case he had any reservations about his skills as a surgeon, she added, "I know ye can do it."

She had more faith than he did. But then he'd learned to be a cynic when it came to medicine. Too many treatments failed. Too many remedies were based on tradition rather than science. He'd learned to keep his expectations low.

Now that Charlotte had seen her damaged ankle, swollen to double its normal size, she began to feel it. It throbbed with every pulse of her heart, and when she tested it, a sharp twinge warned her to keep it still.

She also grew aware of her state of undress. Not only was her frail lawn chemise ripped. It was also indecently sheer.

But propriety was the least of her worries.

At least the ship hadn't capsized. And now that Mr. Jameson was safe and whole before her, tending to her and Campbell, she regretted her verbal fisticuffs with him earlier. He might be a gifted libertine. But he was also a gifted surgeon.

"How are the rest o' the crew?" she asked as Mr. Jameson cleared out a spot on the deck to sit cross-legged.

"No one was lost," he said.

Charlotte breathed a sigh of relief. "And the ship?"

"She needs minor repairs. But we'll know more at daybreak."

He picked up Campbell and set the dog carefully on his lap. Leaning the animal against his inner thigh, he turned him so that his injured leg was uppermost.

Then, he picked among the shards of the broken lantern until he found two pieces of the smooth-edged wood frame.

"What are ye doin'?" she asked.

"Makin' a splint. I'll put these on either side o' his leg and wrap it to keep the bone straight."

"'Tis what I do to my *Orchidicaea*," she marveled, "to keep them growin' straight."

"Exactly," he said, measuring the wood against Campbell's leg. "These should do," he said. "Now I need a bandage."

She didn't hesitate. "Here," she said, offering him the hem of her chemise. "Ye can tear this."

He frowned at the delicate embroidery. "'Tis too fine for Campbell."

"Nonsense. 'Tis ruined anyway."

"Are ye certain?"

It was on the tip of her tongue to tell him she was sure it wasn't the first lady's chemise he'd torn asunder. But considering his heroics in the storm, she bit back the retort and nodded.

Unfortunately, when he clenched his fists in the fine lawn and wrenched them apart, the garment split, not in a neat few inches along the bottom, but up the front by nearly half a yard.

They both gasped at his faux pas. But then his look of horror suddenly struck Charlotte as hilarious. She burst into laughter. And the more mortified he looked, the funnier it seemed.

"My apologies," he said, which made her giggle even more.

Campbell barked, as if he wished to join in the merriment.

Somehow he managed to tear a modest four-inch strip of cloth from the bottom to wrap neatly around the splints. Though Campbell jerked once or twice in pain, he remained calm and trusting.

When Mr. Jameson placed him gently on his feet again, the pup shook off the trauma of his ordeal and limped off on his new limb to sit beside Charlotte.

"Now your turn," he said.

Distracted by Campbell's procedure, Charlotte had had little time to think about her own injury. But now she shivered in trepidation.

"Cold?" he asked in concern.

"Scared," she replied.

"May I?" he asked, indicating her ankle.

She bit her lip and nodded.

His fingers were gentle as he probed the swollen flesh there and turned her foot this way and that. But it still hurt badly enough to draw a few hisses between her teeth.

"'Tis as I thought," he said, resting her heel in his hand, "a sprain, not a break. I'll wrap it, and ye'll have to stay off of it a while. But it should heal with no complications."

She sighed, relieved. "I suppose ye'll need more o' my chemise?"

"Regrettably. But I'll fetch ye decent clothes from your stateroom and bring them to ye in the hold."

She chuckled. "'Twill doubtless be the first time ye helped *dress* a lass rather than *undressin'* her, aye?"

She'd thought her comment was lightly amusing, given his reputation was no secret. But he seemed to see no humor in it.

His face was grim as he cautiously tore a second four-inch strip from the bottom of her chemise. "'Tisn't the truth, ye know, what they say." He narrowed his eyes at her ankle as he slowly wound the strip of cloth around it. "But I don't expect ye to believe me." He overlapped the fabric, checking to make sure it wasn't too tight. "'Tis an unfounded rumor that's unfortunately grown legs." He tucked in the edges and declared her as well as he could make her for now.

He left then to fetch her a new gown. She remained in the dark with Campbell, forced to reconsider her opinion of the rakish Mr. Jameson. To be honest, she thought, scratching Campbell behind the ears, the stowaway *didn't* behave at all like a scapegrace. He'd been appalled at tearing her garment, and he was fetching her clothing to save her from embarrassment.

It was possible the crew had exaggerated his sexual exploits. But what about Lady Adams? What reason would she have to lie?

When he returned, it was in breathless haste.

"Will ye be all right to dress?" he asked, handing her her sarsnet gown of pale green, one blue slipper, and an oar.

"Aye."

"I'm needed in the galley. I'll leave the lantern here," he said, hanging it on a hook in the deckhead. "Take care. Don't put weight on that leg. Use the oar as a crutch. And don't even think o' climbin' any steps."

He turned to go, then turned back. "Would ye mind keepin' Campbell in your cabin, just for the night? The splinters are treacherous here."

She nodded. After he was gone, she dressed as quickly as she could, given the circumstances. She'd follow Mr. Jameson's instructions as much as possible. But there was no way she wasn't going to investigate the storm damage. Someone might need her help. And she wanted to see what had happened to her orchids.

In Mr. Jameson's absence, she made a unilateral decision. Campbell would stay in her stateroom until his leg healed. There were too many obstacles in the hold that could do harm, not only splinters, but barrels that could crush a wee pup. Besides, it was a dark and gloomy place, not fit for a bright-eyed terrier. Mr. Jameson would just have to contend with those arrangements, for she didn't intend to ask his permission.

The two of them limped across the shadowy saloon unobserved. But when she entered her stateroom, it was pitch black. She'd have to wait until dawn to examine the plants and see how much damage they'd sustained. For now, she was just grateful the windows hadn't broken in the storm. The rug was dry, so no rogue wave had washed away her orchids.

Suddenly she heard a loud uproar from outside her door. A cacophony of men's voices. And the scrambling of feet across the saloon.

The hubbub probably had naught to do with her. But Charlotte's curiosity got the best of her.

"Stay here, Campbell," she said, setting him gently in the middle of the big feather bed. "I'll be right back."

Using the oar, she half-limped, half-hopped toward the galley, where she heard an argument raging.

The door was partly open, and the interior was lit by several lanterns. She peered through the narrow opening. Her eyes widened as she witnessed a horrifying scene.

The chief officer was seated atop a squat barrel. His impossibly crooked right arm was stretched across a chopping block. Several crewmen restrained him. Someone offered him a bottle, and he gulped down several swallows, then grimaced. His face was red, and he was sweating profusely. A crewman shoved a short, thick piece of rope between the officer's teeth. Every few moments he groaned with suffering as he bit down on the rope, kicking his feet against the greasy deck of the galley.

From behind the rope, the chief officer yelled, "Do it quick!" as spittle flew from his mouth.

The cook stepped in front of him, brandishing an enormous cleaver.

"Nay!" bellowed Mr. Jameson. "Put that away, for the love o' Christ!"

Charlotte flinched.

The cook hesitated.

The chief officer screamed again, banging his boot heels against the wood.

"Out o' my way!" the cook shouted.

"Ye bloody butcher!" Mr. Jameson cried, seizing the cook's wrist. "I can fix it! At least let me try!"

They snarled at each other, at an impasse, while the chief officer writhed in pain.

"Fine," the cook decided, wrenching out of Mr. Jameson's grasp. Then he shook the cleaver at the stowaway. "But if ye fail, I'll be usin' this to lop your head from your shoulders."

Charlotte gulped. She was sure she didn't want to see whatever was about to happen. And she was just as sure she couldn't tear her eyes away.

"I'll need ye to hold him steady," Mr. Jameson said. "'Twill hurt like the devil."

The crewmen put their backs into it, Two young lads clung to the officer's legs to be sure he wouldn't slide off onto the slick deck.

"Hold his elbow in place," Mr. Jameson directed. He prodded the man's lower arm repeatedly until he found the spot he sought, a process that made the poor man whimper in anguish. Then he clamped the man's wrist firmly in both hands. "Ready?"

"Aye," the crew replied, bracing themselves.

Mr. Jameson pulled with all his strength, steadily, while the chief officer screamed in agony. After a moment, Mr. Jameson seemed satisfied and released his wrist. "There."

The chief officer slumped in exhaustion on the barrel. He spat the rope from his mouth, breathing heavily.

"Well?" one of the crewmen asked.

The officer scowled. Then he glanced down at his arm. "'Tis straight now, isn't it?" he said in amazement.

"As a rudder," another shipmate said.

"'Tis still broken," Mr. Jameson warned. "But if we splint ye well, and ye don't use it for a bit, ye'll be back to boxin' the Jesuit and gettin' cockroaches in no time."

The men laughed in relief, all except the cook, who probably felt cheated out of a meaty bone to flavor his stew.

While Mr. Jameson fashioned a splint for the chief officer, the rest of the crew dispersed. Quickly, before she could get caught, Charlotte hobbled back to her stateroom.

Campbell, overwhelmed from all the excitement, had fallen asleep where she left him.

Charlotte, just as weary, curled up beside him in her clothes.

But she couldn't drift off so easily. Her brain was spinning with everything that had happened in the last day.

Beginning with her embarrassing discussion with Lady Adams.

Her wretched quarrel with Mr. Jameson.

The destructive and terrifying impact of the storm.

The stowaway's heroism in the face of danger. And his considerable skill as a surgeon.

Her opinion of Mr. Travis Jameson had been vastly changed. No longer able to paint him in broad strokes as a villain, she had to admit he was bright and brave and kind.

An honorable man.

A brilliant physician.

A loyal shipmate.

Whatever wicked secrets lurked in his history, he had shown Charlotte naught but gentlemanly consideration and care.

He deserved her utmost respect.

She vowed she would never utter another unkind word to Mr. Jameson.

Indeed, she fully intended to forgive him the indiscretions of his past.

Many voyagers traveled to America to make a new beginning, to embark upon a new life. And so it must be for Mr. Jameson. She'd allow him to start with a clean slate, to become a changed man.

This time when she stroked Campbell's soft fur and closed her eyes, she was filled with new purpose. Her spirit at peace, she finally drifted off to slumber.

That peace was interrupted just before dawn, when she was awakened by Campbell's soft whimpering. She

cracked open one eye and saw he'd managed to clamber down from the bed and was scratching at the door.

"What is it, lad?" she croaked.

Campbell continued to whine until Charlotte at last capitulated, rising with the sun to open the door for him.

Before she could catch him, he ran off.

"Where the devil are ye goin'?"

Neglecting her orchids for once, she worked her foot into her one blue slipper, grabbed the oar, and limped off after the runaway terrier. She feared he might leap off the ship and prayed he wouldn't take the steps to another deck where she couldn't follow.

CHAPTER 7

Travis was dead tired. He'd spent the first half of the night fighting the storm and the second half repairing its damage. By virtue of the fact he had saved the chief officer's arm, the man had told him to take the day off and sleep for as long as he liked.

But his dog had other plans. By the time the sun started to peer through his porthole, Campbell came scratching and whining at the hold door.

Travis rolled out of the hammock and stumbled to the door, cursing as his bare foot caught a stray wood splinter among the wreckage.

He extracted the sliver, and then opened the door.

His scruffy canine patient wagged his tail in greeting. Thankfully, it looked like his splint had held.

But Campbell didn't rush in to the hold. He simply waited expectantly at the door.

"What?" Travis snapped, running a weary hand through his tangled hair.

Then he noticed his second patient hobbling toward him with the aid of an oar, wearing her soft green gown and one blue shoe.

Travis straightened and cleared his throat, smoothing his rumpled slops.

"Miss de Ware."

"Ye must call me Charlotte," she said, surprising him. "Please."

"Charlotte," he repeated. Her name was as lovely as she was. She still had a bit of crusted blood on her brow. But her color was much better today. And she seemed to have mastered the oar as a crutch. Temporarily distracted by his role as a physician, he almost forgot his manners. "And ye—ye must call me Travis, o' course."

"Travis."

He realized she was the first person in a long while who'd called him that. To his friends, he was Jameson. To his patients, Mr. Jameson. And the ship's crew seemed determined to address him as Sawbones, despite his demonstrated distaste for amputation.

He decided he rather liked the sound of his name on her lips.

"How are ye feelin'?" he asked.

"Remarkably well." Her blue eyes sparkled like the sun-tipped ocean. "But I'm afraid this wee lad missed ye terribly."

Travis shook his head at the dog. "Foolish, faithful pup. Ye'd rather languish in the dank hold with me when ye could spend the night on a soft feather bed?"

"I fear he prizes loyalty over luxury and won't stay where he's put as long as his master isn't there," she said, clucking her tongue.

Travis furrowed his brow. He hated to inconvenience Miss de Ware—Charlotte, he corrected—by making her keep the dog in her quarters. But he'd need to thoroughly sweep the splinters of wood and glass from the deck of the hold before it was safe to let Campbell return.

Before he could tell her he'd start on the task straightaway, she added, "And so I believe ye should share the stateroom with us."

She might have knocked him over with a feather. Dumbfounded, all he could manage was, "I beg your pardon?"

"A curtain is already hung in the cabin," she said, "so ye needn't worry about privacy. Ye can sleep on the settee or hang your hammock from the deckhead. Campbell will have a safe place to stay while his injury heals. And the poor pup won't be hobblin' all o'er the ship, tryin' to find his master. So...are ye agreed?"

She made it sound like a practical solution. Almost. Until he thought about the consequences.

"Absolutely not," he decided.

"What? Why?"

"Ye said it yourself," he said. "A man o' my reputation—"

"Piffle! Ye said the rumors weren't true. And I believe ye."

Travis had learned long ago that the crisis of a life-threatening illness—or in this case, a life-threatening storm—made a person feel helpless. And when patients felt vulnerable, they were kind, forgiving, generous. Sometimes *too* generous.

So it seemed with Charlotte. She'd apparently forgotten their disagreement and forgiven him for his sins.

Her words and her trust affected him more than he expected. But he still couldn't let her hasty, heartfelt offer compromise her own reputation.

"*Ye* may believe me," he told her, "but no one else does."

"I don't care," she declared with a cocky tilt of her chin. "My father is Sir Charles de Ware. Nobody would dare question the reputation of a de Ware."

He smiled and shook his head. Her confidence was engaging and amusing. He wondered if the esteemed and no doubt protective Sir Charles de Ware would find it so.

"I insist," she insisted. "And if ye won't agree, then I'll have the chief officer hang an extra hammock in the hold, and I'll join ye there."

A laugh burst out of him. The lass was certainly a bossy minx.

In the end, she won the argument. Somehow, the way she explained it to the captain made him agree to her demands. The chief officer made no protest, mostly because Travis had literally become what he jokingly referred to as his right-hand man. The other passengers, who'd received medical attention from Travis for their bruises and abrasions, restricted their criticism to speculative looks. And whatever conjectures the crew made regarding Charlotte's morals, they were careful not to voice them aloud.

Charlotte's stateroom was luxurious indeed. The cabin was spacious, bright, and airy, with plenty of windows. Of course, her belongings were still strewn all over the deck, victims of the storm. Books littered the floor like stepping stones. Gowns in summery colors flowed out of upended trunks like spent blossoms. But the most surprising thing was the spill of earth and moss from one of the overturned wooden boxes.

"Your orchids?" he guessed, gesturing toward the flowers sprinkled among the dirt.

"Oh no!" she cried, rushing over to them.

"Ye brought them with ye?"

"Aye." She carefully righted the wooden box and began scraping up the dirt, trying to salvage the plants. "'Tis my life's work."

He raised his brows in wonder. "Ye're a botanist?"

"Aye."

"That's why ye wanted to go to Elgin," he realized.

He'd assumed Charlotte merely liked orchids for their beauty. But he should have guessed her true interest when she referred to them by their scientific name.

A curious excitement filled his veins. He'd found a kindred spirit. To discover Charlotte was a woman of science was enticing. It was a rare person who took an interest in science. But even rarer was a scientist who was female.

The surprising Miss Charlotte de Ware was becoming more and more fascinating by the day.

"What can I do to help?" he asked.

"Naught, really. I'll just have to pack them again and hope the roots and rhizomes haven't been too damaged." She sighed, adding, "But my research is ruined."

He knew how she felt. Of course, when one of his subjects was damaged, it ruined more than just his research.

"Please," she said, "make yourself at home. This will take me a while."

He also recognized, though she was too polite to say so, that she didn't want him poking his nose—or his

clumsy fingers—into her research. He understood perfectly. He felt the same way. Research was a solitary pursuit.

The dividing curtain was a sail that stretched from bulkhead to bulkhead and deckhead to deck. On his side of the stateroom was a settee, a dressing table, an overturned chair, a bucket under the table, a wash basin, and two empty trunks. One glance at the short, spindle-legged, silk-upholstered settee convinced him to hang a hammock for sleeping in his half of the cabin. He scrounged up a few rags to toss into one of the trunks for Campbell.

When he was done arranging his quarters, he quietly slipped over to her side. Charlotte was seated on her hindquarters on the deck with a box in front of her and her injured ankle protruding from her gown. She seemed intently focused on arranging the moss-packed plants into their correct spaces in the box, making notations in a notebook beside her.

While she worked, he returned her furniture to its proper place and began restoring the library shelves, arranging the books by subject as best he could.

He was impressed by her collection. She had an enormous tome by Antoine Laurent de Jussieu called *Genera Plantarum*, on the classification of plants. A smaller book by John Ellis gave *Directions for Bringing Over Seeds and Plants, from The East-Indies and Other Distant Countries in a State of Vegetation.* He opened it to discover several illustrations that looked exactly like the trunk Charlotte was repacking. There was also a small, very recent publication, a report on various crops by an organization called the Caledonian Horticultural Society.

Most impressive of all were her two volumes by a scientist whose name he recognized, Carl Linnaeus. He'd only ever seen Linnaeus's important work on taxonomy when one of his patients smuggled it to him from the university library.

These were translations from the original Latin, and it appeared she had only the volumes related to botany. But they were still awe-inspiring to him as he sat on the rug beside the bookshelves, with Campbell dozing beside him, and carefully leafed through the pages.

Linnaeus had been the first to establish scientific terms to classify organisms based on their characteristics, by order, genus, and species. It was this type of classification that had helped Travis identify similar diseases in order to predict their behavior.

As he skimmed the pages, he learned that Linneaus classified plants by a sexual system of organization. A plant's class was distinguished by its stamen or male organ, and the order by its pistil or female organ. He emitted a startled cough, wondering what kind of audacious science the young lass was practicing.

Then his eye was caught by an intriguing passage about leaves serving *as bridal beds which the Creator*

*has so gloriously arranged, adorned with such noble bed
curtains, and perfumed with so many soft scents that the
bridegroom and his bride might there celebrate their
nuptials with so much the greater solemnity.*

Travis raised his brows. It seemed Miss Charlotte de
Ware wasn't quite as innocent as she seemed.

He glanced over at her as she took meticulous
measurements of the plants, recording her findings in
a dog-eared notebook. Her unabashed candor actually
pleased him. A true scientist had to discard modesty,
after all, to look at nature with an unbiased eye.

He closed the book and picked up another—one
devoted solely to orchid taxonomy, *Genera
Orchidacearum,* by a botanist called Olof Swartz. When
he set it on his lap, the book fell open to an illustration.

For one instant, his eyes widened. It appeared to be
an anatomy drawing—one he might find useful in his
own field of study—of the female reproductive organs.

But it wasn't. And when he realized that, he became
even more intrigued.

It was the diagram of an orchid.

He was astounded by the similarity. The botanist
must have been as well, for Swartz gave the orchids
sexual characteristics, even boldly labeling the outer
petals of the flower *labellum.*

Indeed, Travis was so captivated by observing the
parallels between the anatomy with which he was
familiar and the flower's structure, he didn't notice

that Charlotte had finished her work and was standing over him.

"Fascinatin', isn't it?"

He slammed the book shut, waking Campbell.

She gave a little laugh. "Go on," she said. "Ye can read it if ye like." Then, realizing he might be a common surgeon who couldn't read, she added, "Or look at the pictures anyway."

It bothered him that Charlotte assumed he was uneducated. Which was silly, of course. He was accustomed to being underestimated. And it had never bothered him before.

Besides, what reason did she have to think otherwise? He'd been thrown into a crate as a nameless stowaway. The crew called him Sawbones and spread rumors about his debauchery. Most of the medicine Charlotte had seen him employ on the ship relied on skill, practice, and common sense, not book reading.

But he didn't want her to believe he was illiterate. He wanted her to know exactly who he was. As foolish as it might be, he wanted to earn her respect.

So he opened the book again.

"The lateral sepals," he asked, pointing to the petals in the drawing, "are there always two? Or are the variances due to a split in the *labellum*?"

Her eyes lit up. "Come," she said, taking his hand. "Let me show ye."

Half an hour later, he might not have been able to recite back to her all the scientific names of the two dozen orchids of the collection she'd shown him. But he could tell her every subtle hue that gleamed from her pair of beautiful blue irises.

How long had it been, he wondered, since he'd seen a woman through a man's eyes and not a surgeon's? Since he'd looked at a female with anything but clinical interest?

For the last year, he'd been so deeply engaged in his research that women had become mere subjects of study. His natural empathy had been cured early when he began to occasionally lose a patient. Eventually, out of necessity, he'd forced himself to maintain a safe detachment. Aloofness. Distance.

With Charlotte, distance seemed impossible.

Indeed, sitting here so close to her, he was tempted to trespass the mere inches between them and press a soft kiss to her flushed cheek.

But she suddenly exclaimed, "Upon my soul! I've been gushin' like a leaky boat for the last half hour, haven't I? I feared I've bored ye half to death."

"Not at all."

"'Tis just so pleasant to talk to someone who understands—or at least convincingly *feigns* to understand—my passion." She gave him a saucy wink. "But enough about my studies. I fear I've quite monopolized the conversation." She hobbled to her chair. "What about ye? How did ye come to be interested in medicine?"

He started to answer, and then noticed her bandages looked a bit snug. He dragged one of the small trunks over. "If ye elevate the sprain, 'twill keep the swellin' down. May I?"

"O' course." She smiled. "Ye know, for an alleged rogue, ye seem inordinately polite."

He gently cupped the back of her bandaged heel and rested it on top of the trunk.

Then he settled back down on the rug. Campbell limped up to him, and Travis scooped the dog up in his arms, giving him a quick scratch and settling him onto his lap.

"I lost my mother five years ago to a virulent cancer," he told her. "I suppose that's why I wanted to study medicine."

"I'm sorry." She looked sincere. "Did ye attend Edinburgh?"

All the best physicians—those with the wherewithal—attended the University of Edinburgh. Travis had neither the funds nor the social standing for higher education.

"Nay, I taught myself."

"Ah. Like me."

Travis frowned. He'd never thought of that. But he supposed it must be true. For a man, attending university was a matter of wealth and position. For a woman, it was an impossibility.

"I had friends at university who lent me their books," he confided.

"I had a father who indulged me," she said.

"When ye're determined, ye find a way."

"So true," she agreed. "Is your specialty cancer then?"

"Aye."

"What type o' cancer?"

He hesitated, not sure how much he wanted to divulge. Then he looked into Charlotte's eyes. The lass was genuinely curious and interested. Though she looked like a wide-eyed, innocent lass, there was a maturity about her that inspired him to be honest with her.

"The same kind that killed my mother," he said. "Cancer o' the uterus."

Her blank pause made him think she either didn't understand the term or believed, as most did, that it was a disease of prostitutes and women of loose morals. Neither assumption was true.

"'Tis a wretched disease," she said without judgment.

He nodded.

"And are ye makin' any progress?" she asked.

Her response made him want to grab her and kiss her. No one ever asked him that. Not even his friends. They only scoffed at his relentless drive to find a cure.

Instead of kissing her, he replied, "Some. But there are...challenges."

"What kind o' challenges?"

"'Tis a disease no one understands. Not even my fellow surgeons." He frowned. "They all think 'tis a...a..." He tried to think of a polite term she would understand.

"A venereal disease, aye? 'Tis the accepted wisdom."

"Aye, exactly. But 'tisn't true," he eagerly insisted. "The disease is an anomaly o' nature, not a failure o' morality. Accordin' to my research, it has naught to do with vice. *Or* virtue. There's no sexual transmission. None detectable at least. It behaves like any other cancer."

He was speaking more frankly with her than he ever had with another person. It was thrilling.

"And ye're determined to prove it," she said.

"I *have* to. Woman are growin' ill. They're dyin'. But they're sufferin' in silence. All because they're too ashamed to seek treatment."

"Like your mother?"

"Aye."

"But ye've found a way to cure them?"

He gave her a discouraged frown. "Not always. But I can treat them. Those women with the courage to come forward anyway."

Charlotte gave a little gasp. Then she furrowed her brow and narrowed her eyes as if she solved a difficult puzzle. "Women like Lady Adams?"

He recoiled with a blink. How had she guessed? He opened his mouth, ready to issue a stern denial. His reputation and his patients' safety depended upon protecting their identities, after all.

"She tried to tell me," Charlotte realized as the memory of her conversation with Lady Adams began to flood her mind. "But I didn't understand."

"She told ye?"

How Charlotte could have so misunderstood the sweet lady's words, she didn't know. But she was mortified to think of how rude she'd been.

"I think she believed I was one o' your patients." She gave Travis a sheepish smile. "She said what ye'd done for her was a miracle. She told me 'twas naught to be ashamed of. And she wanted to assure me o' your discretion."

He nodded. "Lady Adams is a kind soul. One o' my successes. But please say naught to anyone about it. If her husband were to find out..."

"He'd never understand," Charlotte finished, shaking her head. "He'd think his wife had been unfaithful."

"Right. Any man would." He idly pet Campbell's head. "Even the treatments have to be done in secret."

Charlotte's brain was whirling with enlightenment, alive with curiosity. And now that she was able to connect all the facts, she began to wonder about the conclusions she'd drawn.

"Why, Mr. Jameson," she accused, "I'm beginnin' to suspect ye aren't a philanderer at all."

He barked out a self-mocking laugh. "Are ye disappointed?"

"But ye let everyone believe that. The ship's crew. Me. Your mates in Edinburgh. That man who challenged ye to a duel."

"What else was I to do? 'Tis better they imagine I'm *swivin'* all the lasses of Edinburgh than performin' controversial medical procedures on them. Besides, I'd rather take on the guise of a villain than cast shame upon ill and innocent lasses."

It was the most noble thing Charlotte had ever heard. Here was a surgeon who cared so much for his suffering patients that he would stake his own honor and reputation on improving their health.

Her heart swelled until a lump lodged in her throat. Her eyes filled with adoring tears. And then Charlotte did what her father claimed she did best. Acted on impulse.

With a soft, admiring sigh, she leaned down from her chair, placed her hands on either side of his head, and planted a kiss on the good doctor's mouth.

How she expected him to respond, she didn't know. She hadn't thought that far ahead.

What he did was kiss her back.

Capturing her shoulders in his hands, he inclined his head and slanted his mouth over hers. Pressing tenderly at her lips. Again and again.

A faint moan escaped her.

A light growl escaped him.

His lips were warm and slightly wind-chapped. But she could sense desire and hunger on them, An answering vibration coiled within her ears, filling her head with intoxicating need.

Like a bee sampling an orchid, his tongue slipped out to taste her lips. She responded, blossoming beneath his touch, opening to allow him access.

Their tongues met and danced together until she thought she would faint from the intoxication of the nectar he offered.

And then the jealous sea slapped the ship, making it lurch and jarring them apart.

But as she gazed breathlessly into his smoldering eyes, her own eyes glimmered with the birth of lust and the promise of many more kisses to come.

As it turned out, Campbell found sleeping in Charlotte's big feather bed far more comfortable than where he was supposed to bed down.

Eventually, so did his master.

The crew and other passengers grew accustomed to seeing Travis carry her onto the various decks. And she grew accustomed to having him carry her, even after her ankle had admittedly healed.

By day, Travis helped her catalog the progress of her orchids, which helped erase the heartbreak of losing eight of them in the storm. In return, she helped him reconstruct his research notes, since his notebooks had been left behind in Scotland.

By night, since they were both creatures of science, they let their inquisitive natures lead them to experimentation.

Of course, being in polite company, they were discreet about their activities, and, being knowledgeable scientists, they were cautious about their intimacy.

But they managed to conduct a series of amorous experiments that left them breathless with the thrill of discovery.

They completed a thorough exploration of the art of kissing.

They determined the effect of touch on the various surface areas of the body.

Travis assisted her in experiencing the ultimate blossoming of her bud of desire. And Charlotte carefully indulged her own curiosity regarding the mysterious workings of human pollination.

Time passed in a blur of pleasure and enlightenment.

Not in Charlotte's wildest dreams had she imagined she'd fall for a stowaway who had a reputation as a rake.

Never had she thought, among a motley crew of sailors bound for America, she would find a man with whom she had so much in common.

And little did she know that in the span of just six weeks, she'd grow to love an ordinary surgeon so deeply and completely.

CHAPTER 8

Charlotte stared out across the still, gray sea from the weather deck, toward the buildings in the distance. The dull sky was the color of iron, and the clouds hung low on the horizon, as dismal as her mood.

While the other passengers chattered excitedly about finally seeing the last of the seemingly endless and temperamental ocean, Charlotte counted the minutes left with dread.

There weren't enough of them.

In less than an hour, by the captain's reckoning, they'd dock at the port of New York.

Life aboard *The Fortuity* had been an incredible adventure. One Charlotte wished could last forever. Because she couldn't bear to think of leaving Mr. Travis Jameson.

Her throat clogged with unspent tears of sorrow and frustration, for there was naught to be done.

Charlotte was expected to spend Christmas with her mother's cousin.

Travis needed to work his way back to Scotland, which might take years.

Even if, by some miracle, they managed to find their way to each other in Edinburgh, they would never be allowed to marry. He was a common surgeon with a reputation as a scoundrel. She was a gentleman's daughter, expected to uphold the family honor.

Even the arrival of Campbell, hopping merrily up beside her at the railing—his splint long-gone but his gait forever changed—couldn't cheer her on this glum day.

Travis dipped his mop in the bucket of seawater and swabbed the weather deck for the last time since the journey's beginning.

Campbell, who had free run of the ship now, limped across the planks to join Charlotte at the railing. She picked him up, placing a sweet kiss atop his furry black head.

Travis's heart cracked. The sight of the two of them together made his eyes burn with unshed tears.

He'd never felt so devastated. How would he live without Charlotte?

She was beautiful. Brilliant. One of a kind.

But as much as he'd miss the incomparable lass, he feared Campbell would miss her more, for there would be no way to explain to a wee pup why his best friend in the world had abandoned him.

All the breath deserted him. There was no use denying it. Travis had fallen incontrovertibly in love with Charlotte. The disease of love was incurable. And he was sure he would die of it.

Since there was no remedy, the best he could hope for was to treat the symptoms, keep the patient out of pain as much as possible, and give him something to look forward to.

With that in mind, he took one last swab at the deck, poured the remaining saltwater overboard, parked his mop and bucket, and strode across the weather deck toward the woman he adored.

"Elgin," he said by way of greeting.

"Elgin?"

Her false-bright smile belied the sorrow in her eyes. She'd been thinking about their departure as well.

"Elgin," he confirmed. "In a fortnight."

She bit her lip, as if afraid to hope, for fear that hope would be dashed.

"Say ye'll meet me there," he said with reckless confidence.

"But...how?"

"Ye mean to go there with your kin, aye?"

"Aye."

He took her by the shoulders and gave her a grim look. "I'm sure I can find my way. Saturday, two weeks hence. I'll meet ye there. I swear."

She gulped as she met his gaze. There were so many variables, so many unknowns, that the odds of success were impossible to calculate. But he could tell she wanted to believe him.

"Promise me," he insisted.

On the verge of tears, she compressed her lips and nodded.

They stood together at the railing in silent sorrow then—Charlotte, Travis, and Campbell—staring at the approaching city, until Travis was needed to furl the sails and man the capstan.

When they reached the dock, he remained on the ship, holding tight to Campbell, unable to say a formal farewell to the woman who was taking his heart with her. He watched while the sailors unloaded her trunks and ducked away as she briefly perused the ship, searching for one last glimpse of him.

Soon the bustle on the docks distracted her, and she was lost in a sea of people. Only then did he disembark.

The captain, impressed by Travis's seamanship, and the chief officer, thankful for his medical services, immediately forgave Travis his debt for the journey.

Now all Travis had to do was find his Uncle Reginald, start earning return passage, and discover the location of Elgin Botanic Garden.

"Miss Charlotte de Ware?"

The pinch-mouthed woman who spoke Charlotte's name had a severe look about her. Her black hair was streaked with the same gray as her narrowed eyes and the fur of her pelisse.

"Aye, ma'am?" Charlotte was having enough trouble keeping up a happy countenance appropriate to meeting one's kin. The fact that Mrs. Eugenia Smith looked as if she'd just sucked on a lime only made things worse. She had none of the softness of Charlotte's mother, whose twinkly blue eyes and sweet smile could charm a diehard curmudgeon.

"All these..." Mrs. Smith said, indicating Charlotte's trunks with the end of her walking cane. "They're yours?"

"Aye."

"No, this won't do at all." She spoke to a tall, lathy man beside her. "She may keep two of them, no more."

Charlotte was stunned.

The man nodded and began loading her trunk of clothing onto a waiting carriage.

"Wait!" Charlotte cried.

She quickly surmised from Mrs. Smith's hostile expression that there would be no compromise on the number of trunks.

"Please," Charlotte said, pointing to the two trunks of orchids. "Take these."

What she would do without a change of clothing, she didn't know. But her collection of *Orchidicaea* was irreplaceable.

"And please," she added, "take care with them."

He ignored her second request, but at least he didn't overturn the boxes when he hoisted them onto the back of the carriage.

Charlotte, determined to earn the stern woman's favor, gave her a polite smile and asked, "How am I to address ye, ma'am?"

"Rarely," she said with a scowl of disapproval. "But when you must, you may call me Mrs. Smith."

Charlotte blinked. Perhaps things were done differently in America. But in Scotland, a cousin was met with great affection. A kiss on the cheek. Or at least an affectionate clasp of the hand.

Instead, Mrs. Smith actually poked Charlotte's shoulder with the end of her cane. "Turn around. Let me look at you."

Charlotte was too shocked to respond.

"Turn," the woman repeated, "around."

Charlotte did as she was bid and was appalled when the woman stuck her cane between Charlotte's ankles, lifting her gown up several inches.

"You aren't lame, are you?"

Charlotte flushed. "Nay." She wasn't anymore, thanks to Travis's good care.

Mrs. Smith then scowled into her eyes and said, "And you aren't with child?"

Too stunned to speak, Charlotte shook her head.

"You'll do," Mrs. Smith decided.

Charlotte had never been so mortified. She'd hoped that spending the holiday with kin in America would take her mind off her broken heart. But now she felt like she didn't have a friend in the world.

Once Charlotte's trunks were loaded atop the carriage, the man helped Mrs. Smith into the carriage. But when Charlotte tried to follow her, the woman's cane blocked her way.

"You'll ride on top, with James."

Charlotte's eyes widened. But before she could sputter out a reply, James lifted her up by the waist onto the driver's bench on top of the carriage.

She was still speechless when James sat down beside her, picking up the reins and clucking to the pair of horses to urge them forward.

So upset was Charlotte that she couldn't even enjoy the sights of the city as they traveled down the cobbled streets of New York. The horses clopped past block buildings crowded shoulder to shoulder. Huddled in her pelisse, she shivered, but not from the cold. Dread found its frigid way into her heart. It felt almost like Mrs. Smith was treating her like...

Mustering up her courage, she asked James, "What did Mrs. Smith tell ye about me?"

"You?" he replied. "Not much. Only that you came from Scotland. And your contract is for five years."

Charlotte's knuckles went white where she gripped the edge of the bench. She felt sick. Betrayed. Unable to breathe.

George hadn't sent her to spend Christmas with kin.

He'd sold her as a bloody indentured servant.

It took less than a week for Travis to find his uncle.

It seemed America had looked kindly upon the eccentric Reginald Jameson. *Professor* Reginald Jameson, he corrected. The man's keen interest in natural history had led to a position at Columbia College, where he'd become an esteemed scholar and a well-respected member of New York society.

Once Travis mentioned Reginald's name, he'd been welcomed into the college—and his uncle's household—with open arms.

Travis could not have been more delighted. Americans apparently didn't draw the same distinctions between surgeons and physicians. A man was judged by his talents and his intellect, not by his birthright.

Once he spoke to his uncle about his research into uterine cancer, the professor quickly found him colleagues with whom he could discuss and debate his findings. He learned about a groundbreaking surgery done in America a year ago by Ephraim McDowell, a former student of the University of Edinburgh, in which a cyst was successfully removed from the uterus of a patient.

Within another week, his uncle, impressed by his lively interest, dedication, and meticulous notes, secured a place for Travis among the medical students at Columbia.

He couldn't wait to share his good fortune with Charlotte.

Saturday finally came, the day they were to meet at Elgin Botanic Garden. He got there at the crack of dawn, though he knew it would probably be hours before Charlotte arrived.

Even Campbell seemed to sense his excitement as they ambled along the paths of young saplings. The wee terrier romped about, wagging his tail, and even barking a few times as Travis softly whistled a chanty he'd learned aboard *The Fortuity*.

Midday came and went. Travis's heart leaped every time he saw a dark-haired woman in a fur-lined pelisse stroll past. But it was never Charlotte.

It was the middle of the afternoon when Travis shared the bread, cheese, and apple he'd brought with Campbell. The terrier's enthusiasm had waned. After taking one last bite of cheese from Travis's fingers, he circled and settled on the grass for a nap.

Travis watched the sun go down and the stars come out before he finally accepted that Charlotte was not going to show up.

She'd probably come to her senses, living in a fine house with her mother's cousin. Now that she'd returned to the bosom of her family, she'd probably realized she had no business trafficking with a common surgeon, especially one with a reputation like his.

She was right. He wasn't good enough for Miss Charlotte de Ware. He'd been fooling himself, thinking otherwise.

But it was with a sad sort of irony that he realized he had *become* good enough for her. Leaving his reputation behind in Scotland, he'd become a new man in America. A man of respect. Of social standing. And eventually, of wealth and property.

Still, she had made her choice. Indeed, he expected her mother's cousin was tempting Charlotte with all sorts of eligible dandies who'd been born with prestige and titles. It made him feel ill. But it didn't surprise him.

He hoped one of them would take her to see Elgin eventually. It had been her dream, after all.

With a heavy heart, he scooped up Campbell, tucking the terrier under his coat, and trudged home.

Charlotte wept silently into her work-chapped hands. She perched on the edge of the straw-stuffed pallet in the tiny room that had become her place of refuge. The stars outside her window doubled in her tear-filled eyes as she thought about the hero she'd never see again.

She wondered if he'd gone to Elgin today. Waited for her. Left when she didn't show up.

He'd never find her. No one would ever find her. She was invisible now. Untraceable. A servant without a last name. Without a family.

She dabbed at her eyes with her apron. She needn't have worried about losing her gowns, as it turned out. She'd been given the castoff clothing from the previous servant. A servant, Mrs. Smith was irritated to inform her, had died before her contract was up.

Charlotte's only joy was tending to her *Orchidicaea.* She no longer had time to keep scientific records on their growth. Mrs. Smith kept her employed from dawn to dusk. But she watered them carefully and let them take turns absorbing the sunlight that seeped through her small southern window.

She wondered if they would last as long as her term of indenture.

Sometimes she wondered if *she* would last through her indenture.

She fell asleep that night, dreaming about leaving her tiny room forever and finding her way to Elgin Botanic Garden.

She awoke the next morn—and every morn for the next two weeks—to begin again her regular daily chores of helping the lady to dress, serving meals, and completing the endless tasks that kept a manse of such enormous proportions clean.

The de Ware family home was just as large. But they had an entire staff to manage it. Their servants were provided with comfortable rooms and decent food. They were paid a salary. They didn't have to live on table scraps and castoff clothing. And they didn't have to labor for five years to earn their freedom. Four years, eleven months, and three days, she corrected.

Just before breakfast, while Charlotte was violently polishing the silver and staring at the falling snow, imagining the revenge she'd exact on her brother, if and when she finished her prison sentence, Mrs. Smith called her aside.

It was Christmas Day. Mrs. Smith had a parcel wrapped in brown paper.

How Charlotte could have overlooked the date, she didn't know. After all, she'd been decking the mantles with evergreen boughs, hanging mistletoe, and placing ornaments on the gigantic fir tree in the middle of the salon for a week.

Perhaps she had blocked it from her mind, knowing it would only remind her of the Christmas she was missing with her family.

"As you know, I'm having guests for supper this evening."

"Aye, ma'am."

Mrs. Smith had told her that when Mr. Smith was alive, he'd financially backed exploratory expeditions all over the world. Every Christmas, he sponsored a supper for his beneficiaries, mostly so he could hear tales of their findings. She had continued that tradition, though she admitted her donations were not quite so foolishly generous.

"This is for you," Mrs. Smith said, handing her the package.

Charlotte blushed at the unexpected gift, for she hadn't gotten anything for Mrs. Smith.

"I want you to wear it this evening," she explained, taking the edge off of Charlotte's embarrassment. She looked at Charlotte's frayed apron with scorn. "I can't have you wearing that filthy thing."

An apron. It was a new apron. Of course.

"Thank ye, ma'am."

Charlotte donned the new garment, which was as white as the snow outside. She resumed her duties, trying her best to keep it clean.

To her surprise, as the hour advanced, Charlotte began to look forward to the supper. Mrs. Smith hadn't received guests in all the time she'd been there. It would be pleasant to see new faces. And if the guests brought tales of adventure from all over the world, it might prove an entertaining evening indeed.

She was reminded of the exciting tales she'd heard from her grandfather when she was a young lass. Though she was certain half of them were invented, every orchid he'd brought to her had come with its own origin story.

Suddenly feeling impulsive and inspired by the festive spirit of Christmas, Charlotte hurried to her room. Perhaps Mrs. Smith's guests would be impressed by her collection of exotic blooms.

She'd just finished tucking the last orchid among the sprigs of holly on the table when the first guests arrived.

Travis wasn't stubborn about many things. But he refused to leave Campbell alone on Christmas.

He wasn't particularly keen on going to a withered old widow's supper anyway. Wearing an ascot and tails and trudging through the sludgy snow wasn't his idea of an enjoyable evening.

But Uncle Reginald had insisted. He said the host family had historically given generous contributions to

several professors at the college, funding their research. It would serve Travis well to befriend those kinds of benefactors.

So Travis had surrendered. But he'd insisted, if he had to go, then so would Campbell.

To his credit, Campbell had been an absolute gentleman all day. He hadn't barked at the neighbor's cat. He hadn't brought a dead mouse into the house. And he'd scratched at the back door when he needed to relieve himself. Every time.

So the three of them bundled up for the snow and traveled across town to the oversized gray stone mansion that dominated the block.

Reginald rapped the heavy brass knocker three times. A man in crisp livery answered the door. He lowered a brow in disapproval as he saw Campbell tucked into Travis's coat.

"May we?" Reginald prompted with a growl. "It's damned cold outside."

The man, startled, opened the door wide.

The entryway teemed with guests carrying on lively conversations. They were slowly inching their way into the drawing room, where Travis could hear a string quartet playing Christmas songs.

Reginald went in first, handing the man his hat and greatcoat and greeting a fellow professor he recognized.

Travis was just stomping the snow from his boots when Campbell let out a sharp bark and leaped out of his arms. The terrier slipped through the door, past the servant, and into the crowd.

"Campbell!"

Before Travis could stop the bloody beast, Campbell began squirreling his way between the guests' legs, causing more than a few feminine shrieks. His snuffled his way madly around the entryway, hot on the trail of some invisible prey. Then he bolted into the drawing room.

Reginald shook his head, glowering at Travis.

Travis muttered a curse under his breath, along with a prayer that the hostess didn't own a cat. This was the last time he'd trust Campbell's good behavior.

Somehow Travis managed to squeeze his way through the milling guests in the entryway and the drawing room. For a moment, he lost sight of the wretched animal. Then he heard a few startlingly dissonant violin notes and knew Campbell was to blame.

Finally Travis spotted the dog sniffing intently along the edge of the room. Stealing up on the runaway, he was able to corner him by the fireplace.

With a crow of triumph, he swept the mischievous mutt into his arms. As he held tightly to Campbell, fighting the dog's efforts to squirm free, his eye was caught by the greenery gracing the mantel.

Tucked into the traditional evergreen bough was a trio of exotic yellow blooms with maroon markings.

A curious frisson of recognition shivered through him.

"*Oncidium altissimum,*" he murmured. Why he remembered that, he didn't know.

He turned toward the quartet of musicians playing "God Rest You Merry Gentlemen." On a table beside the cellist, slipped into a vase full of ivy, was a cream-colored orchid with brown spots.

The music seemed to fade as the strange humming in his ears grew louder.

He peered into the adjoining dining room, where the table was set for dinner. Amidst the linen, china, crystal, and silver, strewn among the garlands of holly, were more orchids of yellow, lavender, and white.

Campbell started bucking wildly against his grip, and Travis frowned down at the dog, commanding him to be still.

Then he lifted his eyes again. Behind the dining table, in a servant's apron, looking as pale as a *Vanilla planifolia,* stood the most beautiful flower of all.

Charlotte.

His heart slowed.

The music disappeared.

Time stopped.

Then Charlotte dropped the pitcher she was holding. It shattered on the marble floor, bringing instant silence to the room.

Taking advantage of Travis's loosened grip, Campbell wriggled free and bolted across the dining room. His tail wagging madly, he jumped up on Charlotte, nearly knocking her over in his enthusiasm.

Travis too forgot his manners.

Still in his snow-covered greatcoat, he charged across the room.

Swept Charlotte into his arms.

And vowed he'd never let her go.

EPILOGUE

Travis purchased her indenture that very night, of course.

Charlotte said it was the best Christmas gift she'd ever received.

He insisted he'd done it for Campbell, since the wretched mutt wouldn't let him rest until he fetched her home.

Since Travis was forced to use an advance on his wages from the college to fund her freedom, his uncle offered to let the two of them live at his house until the debt was paid.

Reginald instantly adored Charlotte—almost as much as Campbell did. He fawned over her and bragged about her scientific proficiency until the botany department at Columbia finally agreed to let her serve as an assistant to one of the professors.

Just after the New Year, Travis took her to Elgin Botanic Garden, helping her realize her dream. Unfortunately, the plants were completely covered in snow. But he vowed to take her there every month so she could observe their growth.

Meanwhile, Charlotte's orchids continued to thrive in their new environment, lined up along the south-facing windows of Uncle Reginald's house.

She sent word to her parents, assuring them she was safe and happy and letting them know that she planned to be married in the spring to a promising American physician.

Rather than sending back a letter, the de Wares arrived in person, traveling aboard a packet ship very similar to *The Fortuity*. They claimed they had no intention of missing their daughter's wedding.

They brought a sober and remorseful George as well, whom they said was there to fulfill a debt of honor by serving out Charlotte's period of indenture for Miss Eugenia Smith.

Travis and Charlotte spared her parents the awkward details of how they'd met and fallen in love. There was no mention of stowing away or sharing a cabin. America was a place of new beginnings and social equality, and they decided their relationship should be no exception.

The wedding was lovely, modest, and uniquely American as well. The bride's bouquet was naturally comprised of orchids, and she delightedly recited the scientific names of each one to guests who commented on their curious beauty. When the priest grew suddenly dizzy and overheated, it was the groom who interrupted the ceremony, making him sit with his head between his knees while he applied a compress of ice in a napkin to the back of his neck.

The reception was peppered with lively conversations about research projects, maritime travel, botanic and medical discoveries, and the nation's still young democracy.

Though they didn't know it yet, before the following year, the newly wedded couple would give birth to an intrepid lass named Mary, who would grow up to marry her own world explorer, a Mr. Lawrence Hardwicke.

Lawrence and Mary, in turn, would become the proud parents of a daring artist name Mathilda, who would one day set forth from civilized New York on an adventure as a mail order bride in the wild frontier of the West. There she would find a love—as all the generations of her legendary family had—as true as the North Star, as eternal as time, and more precious than gold.

The End

See what's next in
California Legends

"Brilliant romance!"
—*NYT Bestseller Tanya Anne Crosby*

CALIFORNIA LEGENDS

NATIVE GOLD

GLYNNIS CAMPBELL

USA Today Bestselling Author

Eager to keep reading? A sneak peek of NATIVE GOLD, Book 1, appears at the end of this book.

THANK YOU FOR
READING MY BOOK!

Did you enjoy it? If so, I hope you'll post a review to let others know! There's no greater gift you can give an author than spreading your love of her books.

It's truly a pleasure and a privilege to be able to share my stories with you. Knowing that my words have made you laugh, sigh, or touched a secret place in your heart is what keeps the wind beneath my wings. I hope you enjoyed our brief journey together, and may ALL of your adventures have happy endings!

If you'd like to keep in touch, feel free to sign up for my monthly e-newsletter at www.glynnis.net, and you'll be the first to find out about my new releases, special discounts, prizes, promotions, and more!

If you want to keep up with my daily escapades:
Friend me at facebook.com/GlynnisCampbell
Like my Page at bit.ly/GlynnisCampbellFBPage
Follow me at twitter.com/GlynnisCampbell
And if you're a super fan, join
facebook.com/GCReadersClan

Excerpt from

NATIVE GOLD

California Legends Book 1

Sakote had planned to snare a few squirrels today for the evening stew, but he'd left his hunting pouch at the waterfall. He frowned. He'd hoped to avoid places that would remind him of the white woman. But he had to retrieve it. The deerskin pouch was a gift from his father, and the tools in it—the snares, the knives, the mountain hemp line—would take days to replace.

So with a parcel of dried deer meat and a promise to his mother that he'd bring back some woodpecker feathers for her husband's *wahiete*—his ceremonial crown, Sakote set off for the waterfall.

The pouch was where he'd left it, beside the great boulder. But he couldn't help searching the wet banks of the pool, looking for some sign of the woman who'd come here with him. There was nothing. She'd left behind no scrap of cloth, no scent, not even a footprint.

Of course, that didn't mean her spirit was gone. She lingered here still—in the gurgle of water over the stones, so much like her laughter, in the verdant depths of the pool, like her eyes, and in the heat of the sun upon his shoulder, reminding him of the warmth of her arms around him.

"Damn!" There were no words of anger or frustration in Sakote's language, so he borrowed the curse from the white man.

It didn't matter what the elders said, what the dream tried to tell him, how tempting Mati was. He must follow the old ways, the ways of the Konkow, or they would be lost. The white woman showed him another path, a dangerous path, a path he must not take.

The sun continued to blaze upon his back, and he knew a quick swim in the pond would cool his blood. He took off his moccasins, freed his hair, and loosened the thong around his breechcloth, letting it fall to the ground. Climbing to the crest of the boulder, he took a full breath and dove into the shimmering midst of the pool.

The bracing water sizzled over his skin as he plunged deep through the waves. The chill current swept past his body, swirling his hair like the long underwater moss, washing away his thoughts.

He broke the surface and shook his hair back, then swam for the waterfall. It pounded the rock like a

kilemi, a log drum, and made a mist that hid the small cave behind the fall. He climbed out onto the slippery ledge and stood up, easing forward into the path of the fall, where it pummeled him with punishing force, driving white spears into his bent back and shoulders. The pounding awakened his body and challenged him. He slowly raised his head, braced his feet, reached toward the sky with outstretched arms, and withstood the heavy fall of water with a triumphant smile.

Unfortunately, the loud thunder of the fall prevented him from hearing that he was no longer alone at the pool.

Mattie's jaw dropped. Her breath caught.

After sketching miners all morning, she'd decided to make a few drawings of the waterfall. She remembered the way there, and though she might have hoped the Indian would return, she didn't really expect him. The fact that he had indeed come back, and in such bold display, couldn't have amazed her more.

What in God's name was he doing? He stood at the foot of the waterfall, as bare as the day he was born, letting the water beat him within an inch of his life and grinning all the while.

She thought to yell out to him, to reprimand him for such indecent behavior, such outrageous liberties, such flagrant...but then the artist came out in her. She

realized that what she beheld was beautiful, that *he* was beautiful. Watching him in all his naked glory was like witnessing the birth of a god.

She perched on a rock wedged between two trees, hoping the lush foliage and her drab plaid dress would conceal her. She found an empty page and set to work sketching.

He couldn't remain there long, she knew, or else he'd be pounded into the rock. She had to work quickly, penciling in the bare bones and trusting the rest to memory.

Sure enough, just as she finished the roughest of renderings, he brought his arms down through the fall like great white wings and dove into the middle of the pool.

His naked body slicing through the water sent a rush of delicious fire through her. Her pencil hovered over the page. It was wrong, what she did, spying on him and sketching him in his altogether without his knowledge. And yet, she thought, patting a cheek grown hot with impropriety, it felt so right.

He bobbed up and flung his hair back, spraying droplets of water across the rippling surface.

Mattie pressed her pencil against her lower lip.

He swam forward, gliding through the waves as smoothly as a trout. Then he wheeled over onto his back and floated on the surface, boldly facing the midday sun like some pagan sacrifice.

Mattie's teeth sank into the pencil.

She could see everything—the naked sprawl of his limbs, the corona of his long ebony hair, the dark patch at the juncture of his thighs, and its manly treasure, set like a jewel on black velvet.

He was Adam. Or Adonis. He was Icarus fallen from the sky. Hera cast into the sea. As innocent as an angel. As darkly beautiful as Lucifer.

Mattie blushed to the tips of her toes. She most definitely should not be witness to this...this...she had no word for his wanton display, but she was sure it was completely indecent. Still she couldn't tear her eyes away. He was utterly, irrefutably perfect. And looking at him left her faint with a mixture of emotions as dizzying as whiskey and as unstable as gunpowder.

She slid the pencil from between her lips, flipped to a new page, and began to draw. Despite her rattled nerves, her hand was steady, for she captured every nuance of shade, every subtle contour, each flash of translucence, as if the water lived and moved upon the paper. And the man... He was so true to life that she half expected the figure to lazily pitch over and swim off the page.

A fern tickled her nose, and she brushed it back, and then leaned forward to put the finishing touches on the portrait—a few more branches dabbling in the waves, a leaf floating by his head. She decided on the title, scribbling it at the bottom beside her signature.

Just in time. The Indian knifed under, a flash of sculpted buttocks and long legs, disappearing beneath the surface and into the emerald depths.

Sakote saw the movement of branches from the corner of his eye, but gave no indication. If it was a deer, he didn't want to frighten it from its drinking place. If it was a bear, his splashing would scare it soon enough. If it was a *willa*, he'd have to be clever. He floated a moment more, letting the waves carry him gently toward the deepest part of the pool, watching for sudden movements through the dark lashes of his eyes. Then he gulped in a great breath and dove to the bottom, where the water was cold and shadowy.

He came up silently on the concealed side of the big granite boulder and eased his way out of the water and around the rock until he could see what hid in the brush.

Mati.

She wore another ugly brown dress with lines of other colors running through it like mistakes, and her hair was captured into a tight knot at the back of her head. She bit at her lower lip and leaned out dangerously far between two dogwood saplings, shielding her eyes with one hand, searching the pool for him.

Sakote didn't know what he felt. Joy. Or anger. Relief. Dread. Or desire.

Worry wrinkled her brow, and she leaned forward even farther, bending the saplings almost to the breaking point.

"Oh, no," she murmured.

Her words were only a breath of a whisper on the breeze, but they carried to his ears like sad music. Mati edged between the two trees and took three slippery steps down the slope. Meanwhile, Sakote moved in the opposite direction, up the rise. While she scanned the water, he crept behind her, stopping when he found the sketchbook on the ground, frowning when he saw the figure floating on the page.

Now he knew what he felt. Fury. He glanced down at his naked body, at his man's pride, shrunken with cold to the size of an acorn, then at its perfect duplicate drawn on the paper. And he felt as if he would explode with rage.

He must have made a sound, some strangled snarl of anger, for Mati turned. And screamed.

ABOUT THE AUTHOR

I'm a *USA Today* bestselling author of swashbuckling action-adventure historical romances, mostly set in Scotland, with over a dozen award-winning books published in six languages.

But before my role as a medieval matchmaker, I sang in *The Pinups,* an all-girl band on CBS Records, and provided voices for the MTV animated series *The Maxx,* Blizzard's *Diablo* and *Starcraft* video games, and *Star Wars* audiobooks.

I'm the wife of a rock star (if you want to know which one, contact me) and the mother of two young adults. I do my best writing on cruise ships, in Scottish castles, on my husband's tour bus, and at home in my sunny southern California garden.

I love transporting readers to a place where the bold heroes have endearing flaws, the women are stronger than they look, the land is lush and untamed, and chivalry is alive and well!

I'm always delighted to hear from my readers, so please feel free to email me at glynnis@glynnis.net. And if you're a super-fan who would like to join my inner circle, sign up at http://www.facebook.com/GCReadersClan, where you'll get glimpses behind the scenes, sneak peeks of works-in-progress, and extra special surprises!